SPYDER BONES

Gray Door Ltd.

ISBN 978-1-945530-96-8

TABLE OF CONTENTS

CHAPTER ONE:

Look! A Soldier of Light

Aaron stepped out from the army PX. He pulled the small specialist class four insignia pins from the paper bag. There were eight sets on the card. Pulling two from it, he reached up and removed the corporal insignia from his collar and replaced them with the specialist insignia.

Placing the corporal pins on the card where the specialist pins had been, Aaron put it back in the sack and began walking down the sidewalk toward his barracks.

Fort Hood was busy, and he waited as several large trucks moved past before he chanced crossing the street.

The summer of 1969 was beginning as a hot one. The slight breeze barely gave Aaron any relief.

After a short walk, the young soldier stepped inside his barracks. The building was much cooler, and he quickly pulled his hat off. He then passed by the CQ desk and jogged up the stairs to his quarters.

Opening the door, he found a young private standing in the middle of the room, seeming a bit lost. He had his gear and duffle bags all around him and looked surprised when Aaron entered the room.

"Hello, corporal," the private said and then, noticing the specialist insignia, said, "Oh, uhm, I thought this was Corporal Prescott's room."

"I'm Corporal Prescott or was Corporal Prescott." Aaron then extended his hand to the young private.

"Oh, well, it's nice to meet you. I'm Wilson, or Mark Wilson. I mean Private Wilson."

Aaron smiled and briefly recalled his first few months after boot camp.

"Well, it's nice to meet you, Private Wilson. I suppose we're roommates for the time being?"

"Yes, sir, I mean corp... specialist."

"Well, that's good. And the reason my rank changed is that I changed my MOS from cavalryman to combat medic. I recently finished my training, but most of the guys around here have only known me as a corporal."

Private Wilson nodded, but still appeared lost.

"So, you've been over there, right?" the private asked.

Aaron moved over to his locker and opened it. He glanced back at the private and then sat his paper sack on a shelf.

"Vietnam?"

The private nodded.

"Yeah, two years as a cavalryman, and now I've re-upped as a medic."

The young man appeared shocked.

"You re-upped? Really? Why?"

Aaron moved around the private, sat on his bunk, and looked up at Mark.

"I re-enlisted for two more years because I like the army. Is that so surprising?"

"You mean… you weren't drafted to begin with?"

"No, I volunteered."

The private appeared even more astounded. His eyes were wide, and he stared at Aaron.

"If I wasn't drafted, I wouldn't go. I mean, I heard it's really bad."

Aaron smiled. "Oh, it's not bad all the time."

The young private gave him an odd look but quickly recovered.

"So, is that my locker then?" he asked, pointing to the one beside Aaron's.

Aaron nodded and began to help him get settled.

The following day, Aaron and Mark were sitting in the recreation room watching television. Not far from them, several young soldiers played a game of pool.

A husky soldier walked into the room. Upon seeing Aaron, he shouted out.

"Hey, Spider!"

Aaron looked back, and as a smile broke across his face, he jumped up and moved toward the burly soldier.

"Anderson! You…old skunk, what are you doing here?" Aaron then shook the soldier's hand and grasped his arm.

"Oh, I thought I might give the Vietcong another chance to do me in. I don't think they can. But you know me, I'm a betting man!"

Aaron looked at him closely. His face tightened a bit.

"So, it has nothing to do with Hue?"

3

Anderson's eyebrows raised.

"What? Naa, no more than you re-upping has anything to do with Ping."

Aaron smiled. "Actually, Ping has a lot to do with me re-upping, but I'll be sure to tell Hue that she had little to do with you re-enlisting."

Anderson's face turned grim. "You better not, Spider, if you know what's good for you."

Both laughed. Then, Aaron introduced him to Private Wilson. The young private smiled meekly.

"Well, Private Wilson. You should know that Spider here is one hell-uva corporal. I've been through it with this one, and he's the best."

After Anderson said this, Private Wilson replied, "Specialist, you mean?"

Anderson glanced at Aaron's collar.

"What the hell? What's going on?"

Aaron appeared a bit embarrassed. Anderson continued.

"Wait, you did it, didn't you? You went and did it. You changed your MOS, didn't you?"

"Yeah, I told you I was going to," Aaron replied.

"Man, why would you ruin a perfectly good soldier career by becoming a medic? Now, I'll have to call you 'Doc,' or 'Bones,' or something like that. Honestly, I liked you as Spider."

Aaron smiled again.

"I wanted to do something else. Actually, I've been wanting to do it for a while now." He then patted Anderson on the arm. "I'll see you later. I'm sure glad one from our troop came back. I was beginning to think I would be the only one."

Anderson nodded. "Yeah. Well, there's not many wanting to go where we're headed, and even fewer that are crazy enough to go back once they've been there."

With that, Aaron left the recreation room.

Once he had gone, Private Wilson asked, "Why do you call him Spider?"

Anderson chuckled. "That man was the most successful tunnel rat in our unit, private. He would take two Colt 45s into a Vietcong tunnel and clear it out. Then, we would laugh and say he looked like a "spider" when he came crawling back out. So, we started calling him Spider. Make no mistake, private. That's one of the bravest or craziest men you'll ever meet. You did well to end up in a unit with him."

Private Wilson nodded with an impressed expression.

Over the next week, the squad replacement group filled out. Most were new soldiers that had been drafted, though a few volunteered.

There were also a few that had re-enlisted as he and Anderson had done, but in this group, only the two veterans remained. From Aaron's squad, some had been killed, several were wounded and not able to fight any longer, and around half had made it to the end of their enlistment in one piece.

Two weeks later, the cavalry soldiers boarded the first of several long flights and layovers. A few days later, Aaron and his fellow soldiers stepped off the back ramp of a large transport plane and set foot on the southeast Asian soil of Vietnam.

Anderson took in a deep breath and exhaled.

"Mmmm, sweet tropical flowers with just a hint of napalm. Smells like home."

Aaron chuckled as he struggled with the bulky gear and walked past his friend.

"What are you laughing about, Bones? You're glad to be back too. You don't fool me." Anderson said.

Aaron stopped and looked back. "Would you stop calling me Bones?"

"Nope, I've decided you don't look like a 'Doc,' so Bones will have to do."

"I kinda liked Spider," Aaron replied and then began walking again.

Anderson hoisted his duffle bag onto his back and, grabbing his other gear, fell in behind Aaron.

"Yeah, well, I told you not to do that medic thing. You see, that's what happens. You changed your job, and now you get to be Bones instead of Spider. It's not like I didn't warn you."

Aaron glanced back at his friend. He gave him an odd expression but continued his departure from the runway.

The rest of the day was spent getting settled in. The officers were glad to see a few seasoned soldiers among the otherwise green troops.

That afternoon, Aaron and Anderson requested a pass for Saturday, and to their surprise, each received one.

Several days later, the two rode in a taxi to Saigon. Anderson teased his friend along the way.

"I'll bet Ping has forgotten all about you. She's probably already got her another GI. I'm guessing a jarhead or a sailor."

Aaron studied Anderson as the car darted through traffic. The taxi driver laid on the horn and shouted something in Vietnamese to another driver.

"So, you don't think Hue has her another steady?" Aaron asked, once the vehicle seemed to be out of harm's way.

"Oh, I'm sure she does. You see, I've already come to that conclusion. A sweet gal like Hue attracts 'em like honey. But, once she knows I'm back, she'll drop them deadbeats like rotten tomatoes."

"Well, maybe I've come to the same conclusion about Ping," Aaron replied.

"Yeah, right! You can't fool me, Bones. You're ga-ga over Ping!"

"Bones again? Why can't you just call me Spider?"

The taxi swerved again, and both men held the door.

"Nope, you're Bones now. I already told you not to do the medic thing. But no, you had to go and ruin a perfectly good cavalryman to be a medic. So, you're Bones now. Learn to like it."

Aaron grimaced slightly as the small car pulled up to a nightclub. Anderson's attention turned to the music and laughter emanating from within the building as Aaron paid the driver.

When the two soldiers walked into the club, they were met with a thick haze of cigarette smoke and blaring dance music.

Pushing through a mass of American GIs, they came to a large open room. A stage area ran along the walls, and on the

7

stage were beautiful Vietnamese women. They all wore skimpy outfits or bikinis and danced to the music being played.

The men shouted or whistled at the women, and very often, one of the dancers would need to step back as a soldier or marine would try to touch a woman's leg.

Aaron looked through the smoky haze, searching for Ping. Finally, he spotted her on the stage area to his far left. He nudged Anderson.

"Oh yeah! There's Ping. Do ya see Hue?"

"No, but I'll ask Ping about her…if I can get her down from the stage."

As the two came closer to the attractive and petite Vietnamese woman on stage, Ping let out a scream. She began to wave and, moving carefully in her high heels, maneuvered past the other women and then down some steps.

"SPIDER!" She yelled and then pushed a soldier away who was trying to get his hands on her.

Ping weaved through the crowded club and landed in Aaron's arms. She immediately gave him a kiss on the lips and then, pulling away from him, slapped his face.

"Hey," Aaron rubbed his cheek as several soldiers around them, including Anderson, laughed.

"You make me worry, Spider. Where you been? You know I can't wait forever."

"I told you it would be three months, Ping."

As Aaron said this, a Vietnamese man came over and started chattering and pointing up to the stage.

Ping chattered in Vietnamese back to the man, who appeared to be the manager.

"I got to go back work."

"Hey, where's Hue?" Anderson asked as she turned and began to make her way back to the stage.

"She backstage. I tell her you here. She be so happy. We done work in hour. You watch dance. Then, we go to Rosco's."

The Vietnamese manager again chattered something to Ping and pointed at the stage. The pretty Asian dancer chattered back and then made her way back up to the stage.

Aaron and Anderson bought a couple beers and were soon seated below the area where Ping was dancing. Aaron leaned back and smiled as she swayed to the music.

Soon after Ping took her break, Hue came running out in a very skimpy "police-woman" outfit and was hugging Anderson, much to the aggravation of the manager, who again began to chatter in Vietnamese and point to the stage.

Ping came back out in a different skimpy outfit a few minutes later. The two then danced on stage in front of Aaron and Anderson until their shift ended.

The four left the club and were soon packed in the back seat of a taxi headed to Rosco's Place.

Ping sat on Aaron's lap in the small car and snuggled up to him.

"Why you take so long? I may go to other GI if you not come back soon."

Aaron smiled and kissed her neck, causing her to smile.

"I told you, I had some training."

9

At this point, Anderson broke in, "Yeah, he's a medic now, Ping. I told him not to do it."

"You what now?" she asked, looking at him with concern.

"A medic, it's kind of like a doctor."

"You doctor now? Good, you doctor me tonight, sweetheart." She then snuggled him again as the taxi pulled into the lot at Rosco's Place.

Stepping out of the car and into the tropical heat, rock and roll came from inside the club.

After paying the cab driver, Anderson walked over and opened the large Asian-style door. A cloud of cigarette smoke billowed out.

Venturing inside, Aaron spotted a band on stage, one he was familiar with. The band was made up of American "grunts" or foot soldiers and had named the group "Infantry."

This club had a mix of men and women, as opposed to the club where Ping and Hue worked.

As the four made their way closer to the band, which was playing a popular Rolling Stones song, Aaron spotted a table occupied by the group's girlfriends.

They maneuvered to the band's table as the song ended.

"Well, look at this. The cavalry finally showed up!"

Aaron glanced up on stage as the lead singer had obviously spotted the four. He waved at the singer, as they were still trying to reach the table.

"Hey Spider, how's America? We haven't been there for a while now," the singer asked in a monotone voice. Laughter rang out from the crowd as the four finally made it to the table.

"It's still there!" Aaron shouted as he pulled a chair out for Ping. More laughter came from the crowd.

Several attractive Vietnamese women in miniskirts similar to the ones Ping and Hue wore examined them as they sat down at the table.

"Well, that's good to know, Spider," the singer said. He then took a drink of his beer as Aaron sat down.

"Well, now that you've sat down, how would you like to give Joe here a break?"

The singer then turned to the bass player, "You want a break, Joe?"

The bass player smiled. "As long as I can sit with Spider's girl."

More laughter erupted.

"You hear that, Spider? Come on up here so Joe can get some flirting in on Ping."

Aaron glanced at Ping, and she motioned for him to go up.

"Order me a beer, would you?" Aaron asked her as he stood back up.

"Yeah, sure. If Joe no steal me from you!"

Aaron gave her a suspicious glare as he left the table. She smiled seductively.

Joe stepped off the stage and immediately sat down by Ping.

Once Aaron had reached the stage, he squinted from the bright lights, and looking out to where Ping sat, he shouted, "Hey, just talking, Joe. Nothing else!"

There was more laughter as Joe yelled back, "Sure, Spider. Whatever you say, man!" He then put his arm over the back of Ping's chair and leaned over to talk with her.

As soon as Aaron had the strap to the bass guitar over his shoulder, the band started a lively rock and roll tune. The crowd shouted out in approval, and Aaron joined in.

Five songs later, Aaron stepped off the stage and, after some coaxing, managed to pry Joe away from Ping. Joe then stepped back on the stage, and the band began to play again.

Around midnight, the club closed. Aaron, Ping, Hue and Anderson found themselves staggering down the dark street, with a beer in each hand.

Seeing a light on in a shop ahead of them, they walked toward it.

A few seconds later, they found themselves in front of a tattoo parlor. Inside, the Vietnamese tattoo artist was finishing up on a soldier.

"Come on, Bones. Let's get one."

Aaron glanced at his friend. "I'm not getting an army tattoo, Anderson."

"You don't have to. I'll get one. You can get whatever you want, but you said six months ago that you'd get one if I did, remember?"

Aaron grimaced a bit, then tipped up his beer and finished it. Ping immediately handed him an unopened one and, taking the empty, sat it on the ground beside the wall.

"What do you think?" Aaron asked Ping.

"I no care what you do. I not get tattoo. It not good for my work. Not many tips for a tattoo girl."

12

"Come on, Bones. Let's go," Anderson started toward the door.

"Hey, my boyfriend is no Bones. He Spider. You stop call him Bones. I don like it." Ping then followed Hue, who had followed Anderson into the parlor.

Aaron shook his head but followed the other three in.

Ten minutes later, Aaron was sipping his warm beer and watching Anderson get a "1st cavalry" tattoo on his right upper arm.

Since the tattoo Anderson got was common, it didn't take long. Soon, his friend was looking the new artwork over. He then pulled his shirt back on and tapped Aaron's arm.

"Your turn, Bones."

"Hey, it Spider. I tell you already, Andreson!" Ping again protested and then took hold of Aaron's arm.

"Ping, you need to lighten up."

The Vietnamese woman stood up and slapped Anderson's chest, causing him to step back and laugh.

"You lighten up, Andreson!"

After both calmed down, Anderson shrugged his shoulders to Aaron, "Well?"

"Yeah, all right. But I'm not getting a first cav tattoo."

Ping turned to him. "You should get 'Spider' tattoo. I like Spider name."

"No, Bones. You know, with a medic cross!" Anderson said with enthusiasm.

Ping immediately stood up again and slapped him on the arm where he had just received the tattoo, causing him to flinch and put his hand over it.

13

"I toll you, Spider, not Bones!"

Hue laughed at the excitement.

"Ping, it needs to be Bones. He's a medic now."

"No! Spider!" Ping replied with a loud voice.

"Bones!"

"Spider!"

"Bones! Ping, come on!"

"Spider!" she said again.

Aaron sat listening. Then, he held up his hand, and both turned to him.

"How about, Spider Bones, no, Spider, but spelled with a Y instead of an I. Spyder Bones. With a medic cross and a spider web, somewhere on it."

Ping and Anderson looked at each other. Then, they looked at Aaron.

"Yeah, that sounds groovy." Anderson finally said.

Aaron looked at Ping.

"Yeah, that fine. But Spyder first, right?"

Aaron smiled and nodded.

After ten minutes of talking with the tattoo artist, a design was drawn up. It was a medic cross, and in a circular fashion, over the top and bottom were Spyder and Bones. In the corners of the cross, there were spider webs and one small spider.

After another hour in the tattoo chair, the four walked out of the parlor as Aaron pulled his shirt back on.

By now, it was close to 2:30AM. Aaron and Ping parted ways with Anderson and Hue.

On the way to Ping's grandmother's house, she kissed him almost nonstop. On several occasions, Aaron pulled her hand from his crotch as the taxi driver glanced in the mirror.

A few blocks from her grandmother's house, Aaron paid the cab driver as Ping rubbed his buttocks. Turning and walking in the darkness, they made their way along a path through foliage and humid heat to the small house.

Aaron had never asked Ping about her parents or why she lived with her blind grandmother. He wasn't sure if her parents were still alive or if she was just taking care of her elderly grandmother. Ping also never volunteered the information.

As they crept closer to the house, both became hushed, to avoid disturbing her grandmother.

Slowly, they moved toward the small structure, which had only a dim light shining in the front.

When they were about twenty feet from the house, a voice came from the darkness.

"Nghe này, một người lính của ánh sáng đến gần. Cái ác sẽ sợ và qua đời sẽ rơi vào quỷ bóng tối ai dám trespass. Là các quân nhân dũng cảm của ánh sáng, phải dũng cảm."

Both stopped in their tracks. It was Ping's grandmother. Suddenly, Aaron recalled that she said this every time he came to the house. He had asked Ping about it before, but she would never tell him what her grandmother was saying.

Now, Ping took Aaron by the hand and walked to the house. She greeted her grandmother, who was sitting outside in the dark, and then led Aaron through the house and to her small room in the back.

"What did she say?" Aaron asked as Ping closed the door behind them.

"It nothing. No worry. She a little crazy is all."

Ping then grabbed Aaron's crotch and began to kiss him again. With some effort, Aaron pulled Ping from him.

"No. Wait, Ping. I've been away for over three months. You said your grandmother is blind, which I believe because we just walked up in almost total darkness. But your grandmother says the same thing every time I come to this house. Now, I need to know what she's saying."

Ping huffed. She then moved over and clicked on a small, dim lamp that sat on a table beside her bed.

She stared at Aaron for a few seconds, then replied.

"Spyder... I tell you already. She a little crazy. Just forget it." She then moved over and again reached for his crotch.

Aaron caught her hand before she took hold of him.

"Ping, I really want to know. You always put me off when I ask you. I want to know."

The Vietnamese woman grimaced, then ran her fingers through her jet-black hair.

A few seconds later, she pulled the straps of her short outfit over her shoulders. Then, she pulled it down to reveal her breasts.

"Don you want to know about these? You been gone for long time. Don't you miss these?"

Aaron glanced at her exposed breasts. He smiled slightly.

"Ping, you're stalling."

"Aaahhhggg," she pulled her dress back up over her breasts. "You American, why you must know everything?"

16

As she sat on her bed, Aaron raised his arms, "I don't want to know everything, sweetheart. It's just that every time I come here your grandmother says the same thing. Now, how does she know it's me, and why does she say the same thing? If it happened to you, wouldn't you be curious?"

Ping glanced up to him. She frowned but then said, "Look, Spyder, my grandmother was some kind of... I don know how to say."

Aaron thought about it. "What?"

Her face twisted in thought. "I don know. She...when she was young, she, see future things. The people, they pay her to see these future things."

"You mean, like a fortune-teller?"

Ping's face again twisted. "I don know what you say. She just sees things, like future things, things in spirit world. This is how she make money. She tells people what things they can do to stop from being hurt and things like that."

Aaron considered this.

"So, what's that got to do with what she's saying?" Aaron asked.

"It just crazy talk. I think she just talking like she is telling someone things from when she tells future things."

Aaron studied Ping. She looked at him and grunted with frustration.

"Nghe này, một người lính của ánh sáng đến gần. Cái ác sẽ sợ và qua đời sẽ rơi vào quỷ bóng tối ai dám trespass. Là các quân nhân dũng cảm của ánh sáng, phải dũng cảm.

"It mean, like, uhmm... Look! A soldier of light come near. Evil surely fear and death fall on dark...uhm... demons that... uhm, who dare trespass. Be brave, soldier of light. Be brave."

Aaron examined Ping. She looked at him.

"It crazy talk. I tol you. Right?"

For several seconds Aaron considered what she said. Ping watched him closely. Then, he turned to her.

"What were you showing me a few minutes ago?"

Ping gave him a sultry smile and pulled her dress down again. Soon, they were making love.

CHAPTER TWO:

Valley of the Dead

The following week, Aaron found himself in the jungle, getting shot at by the Vietcong. Initially, he had the urge to shoot back, but he soon adjusted to his new role as a combat medic.

While not in the field, Aaron tended a variety of wounds and ailments.

He always looked forward to time off and seeing Ping again. He would spend hours watching the exotic Asian beauty dance. Then, they would go to Rosco's Place, where he would often stand in for the bass player of the regular band. Afterward, they would try to sneak into her grandmother's house. Regardless of it being day or night, the blind elderly Asian woman would greet him with the familiar, though cryptic, greeting.

Before he knew it, his leave or pass would be over, and he would be back in the thick of a firefight.

"You got a smoke, Bones?" Private Wilson glanced at Aaron and then refocused on the dense jungle in front of him.

"I don't smoke."

"Oh yeah," the young private replied, and then lifted his M-16 up a little higher, as if ready for anything.

"Since when did you start smoking?" Aaron asked the young man as they pushed through a leafy bush.

"A few weeks ago."

"Well, I don't think it's very good for you," Aaron replied.

"Maybe not but getting shot at ain't either."

Aaron smiled a bit, "I suppose that's true."

They walked for another five minutes. Suddenly, bullets began to fly all around them. Immediately, the soldiers dropped to the ground. The men in the forward positions began to return fire.

Aaron crawled over to a young private who had been hit in the leg. He was holding it and rocking back and forth in pain.

As Aaron began to help the wounded soldier, he could hear the lieutenant calling for air support on the radio.

Leaves and brush from the trees above fell all around as the bullets continued to pierce the air.

The lieutenant turned and yelled to a soldier with the grenade launcher, "In sixty seconds, plant a couple smoke grenades in their position. I don't want them bastards to have time to get out! Air support will be here any time now!"

Aaron glanced over to the soldier, who nodded and began loading a smoke grenade in the launcher.

In the forward position, the chattering of the M-60 machine gun began to sound off.

Aaron patted the wounded man after giving him a shot of morphine and quickly putting a bandage on his leg. He then began to crawl over to another wounded soldier who was calling out for a medic.

As he pulled a bandage pack from his gear, he could hear the grenade launcher going off with a "phthunk." Four times the soldier launched smoke grenades into the enemy's lines.

The bullets stopped just about the time he could hear the Hueys flying toward them.

Staying low, Aaron crouched over the soldier, who was now almost screaming in pain. The choppers flew overhead and launched rockets into the enemy positions. Then machine gun fire came as the Huey gunners strafed the area.

It was a long day as he and the wounded were evacuated from the area by helicopter. Back at the base, he continued to administer aid. An hour later, more of his comrades arrived. They had continued the firefight after he left and, along with a medic who stayed, were finally airlifted out of the area.

Around 10:00PM, Aaron shuffled through the humid night air and finally reached his tent. Anderson was laying on his cot but leaned up on his elbow as Aaron pulled some clothes from his locker.

"Burning the midnight oil?" Anderson asked.

Aaron threw a towel over his arm and, along with his clothes and shaving kit, turned toward the door.

"Yeah, and then some," he replied.

"Hey," Anderson said just before Aaron left the tent.

"What? I need a shower and some sleep."

"It was like the Vietcong was waiting for us today. It's like someone is telling them where we're going to be, and they just wait for us. You know what I mean?"

21

Aaron nodded his head a little. "Yeah, I agree. But don't look at me. I didn't tell them."

He then walked outside into the dark and toward the dimly lit showers. Anderson lit a cigarette and laid back on his cot.

The following weekend, the two were sitting at a table in front of the stage where Ping and Hue danced.

Aaron finished the remainder of his beer. He then looked up and smiled at Ping as she swayed about and watched him. Soldiers yelled out and whistled at the barely dressed dancers on stage.

A few hours later, they were at Rosco's Place. Later, Aaron rented a room for the night, as they didn't want to go all the way back to Ping's grandmother's house.

This routine continued for seven months. It was a strange existence that revolved around danger, death and love. Aaron thought little about other things. He survived to spend another weekend with Ping. He seldom considered the possibility of everything changing. But it soon would.

"Damn, it's hot here!" Private Wilson wiped the sweat from his forehead and then put his helmet back on.

Aaron nodded but kept his eyes on the trees that were about thirty-five yards on the other side of the field they were moving across. He didn't like the situation. He could see the lieutenant ahead, and he seemed nervous.

"Don't you think it's hot, Bones?" Wilson persisted and then took a seemingly desperate drag from his cigarette.

"Yeah, it's hot," Aaron replied, still scanning the woodland area across the field.

"Shh. Keep it down back there." The lieutenant then motioned with his hand behind him.

This was a bad place to be. Aaron felt his stomach turn as they continued across the field. He hated these situations. It was way too…out in the open.

Cautiously, they continued toward the woodlands on the other side.

Then, he heard a "phlunnk" sound. He knew what it was and dropped to the ground just as the bullets started to fly. The lieutenant yelled, "HIT THE DIRT!"

Private Wilson was hit in the leg and the arm before he could get down. The split second of Aaron knowing the sound of a mortar shell being dropped in the tube and Private Wilson not knowing, was the difference between getting shot and not.

As the bullets took down five or six men, the mortar rounds began to fall.

Explosions rocked the earth Aaron was attempting to claw into.

There were not many low spaces, but Aaron managed to slither to a lower area.

An M-60 machine gunner began returning fire. Men were screaming, and Aaron quickly counted seven wounded.

As the return fire slowed the enemy's mortar attacks, Aaron moved over to Private Wilson and took hold of his uniform. He was screaming out in pain. Aaron pulled him over to the low area.

"Where's my gawd damn M79? Can someone plant some grenades on them bastards?" The lieutenant yelled out just before another mortar shell landed close by.

Aaron left Private Wilson and crawled over to where the M79 gunner had been. He found half of him lying face up, dead eyes staring into space.

Fortunately, the mortar round had not destroyed the grenade launcher. Aaron quickly pulled it from the dead soldier, along with his ammo bag.

As fast as he could, Aaron loaded the weapon and soon had a grenade headed to the wooded area across the field. He loaded another round and another. As they hit, he adjusted his aim to where he thought the enemy mortars were.

"I need air support at whiskey 527, repeat whiskey 527. We have casualties. We need fire support and med-evacs!" The lieutenant was almost shouting on the radio as Aaron continued to fire the M79.

As more soldiers fired into the woods and more grenades landed in the enemy's positions, the return fire slowed.

Soon, they heard the Hueys, and the enemy seemed to back away. As the air support fired into the woods, Aaron began tending to the wounded.

Sporadic small arms fire came into the area as several helicopters landed to extract the wounded.

Anderson was firing his M16 into the woodlands to keep the Vietcong from attacking again.

Smoke drifted around the men. Aaron came to Private Wilson. He had lost a lot of blood and was fading out.

More helicopters came in and landed.

"Everyone out! Get the hell out! We'll let air support clean them bastards up!" the lieutenant yelled out as the others loaded into a Huey.

Aaron lifted Private Wilson and carried him over to a Huey. Enemy bullets hit several spots on the helicopter as Aaron hoisted the young man up. A crewman helped Wilson into the last available seat.

"Come on!" the crewman yelled.

Aaron jumped up on the skid and leaning half in and half out of the chopper. It lifted off. Vietcong bullets hit the skid of the helicopter, coming very close to Aaron's foot. The Huey gunner sprayed M-60 machinegun fire around the woodlands.

The Huey climbed higher into the air. Aaron glanced back and saw another helicopter about twenty yards away. The machine gunner was also laying down a stream of M-60 rounds into the wooded area.

Private Wilson began to stir. He moaned from the pain and moved to his right, almost pushing Aaron out of the helicopter. He took hold of the seat and tried to shift over some. Bullets again hit the helicopter. Aaron could see in the cockpit, and as he was trying to get a better hold, he saw one of the pilots get hit. The pilot slumped to the side, and the helicopter suddenly leaned. Aaron lost the slight grip he had on the seat and fell backward from the Huey. His heart began to race as he and the helicopter separated.

Arms flailing about, he seemed to be falling slowly as his mind raced. In these brief seconds, he did something extraordinary. He somehow leaped from himself, just as his body impacted the ground.

How he did it, Aaron didn't know, but as soon as he hit the ground, part of his body, the upper part, was somewhere else.

His heart beat fiercely as he seemed to be half on the ground in Vietnam, and half in a place he could barely comprehend.

Looking around, it was as if he were hanging from his midsection on a massive glimmering wall. He could see the other part of his body through this strange glistening barrier, but he was caught between the two places.

Aaron looked down and suddenly became even more frightened. Below was what could only be described as a nightmarish hell. There were black, evil-looking lizard creatures eating and fighting over what appeared to be bodies of people.

Then, to his side, something began to slip through the glistening wall. Aaron felt nauseous as what appeared to be a rotten and diseased person slithered through the barrier. The person looked to be alive, though only barely. Then, Aaron realized it was a soldier from his unit. The man was not a friend of his, but he could see it was him.

As the man's dying eyes stared at Aaron, his black and infested body fell through the wall and then onto the bottom where the grotesque demon-looking creatures waited. As soon as the body landed, the creatures began to devour it.

Aaron tried to move through the wall and back to the world he knew, but he was stuck. As he struggled, farther away from him, a bright light burst through the wall. It shot like a bolt of light across the area and above the demon creatures.

As Aaron watched, he noticed strange beasts and beings flying about in what looked to be the sky, though there was no sun or clouds to be seen.

From what he could see, there were two types of creatures. One was radiating light and appeared to have shining armor. The other was a dreadful-looking black creature with the appearance of a gargoyle.

These beings flew about and often attacked one another in midair. The strangeness again caused a streak of fear to strike his heart. Aaron once again tried to move through the glimmering wall.

As he looked to where his lower body and legs would be, on the other side of the odd, shimmering barrier, he observed soldiers picking him up. Behind them were several more Huey helicopters.

As they carried his body to the chopper, a thin thread-like substance streamed away from the wall. It was as if a thread of his clothing was attached to the part of him that was on the other side of the wall, spooling out as the soldiers carried him.

Again, he struggled in his apparent trapped situation. Then, a large, hideous gargoyle creature landed about fifteen feet from him.

Aaron's eyes widened as the creature stared at him, then began to walk, as if it were not sideways but walking on a floor or the ground.

The creature extended its arms and claws to take hold of Aaron. Suddenly, one of the light-radiating beings landed in front of Aaron. With one stroke of a shining sword, the being sliced the gargoyle in two, and it fell to the hellish depths below.

The being then turned and examined Aaron closely. It was the most beautiful woman Aaron had ever seen. He thought for certain this must be an angel. She had wings and wore a golden set of armor.

As she leaned closer and studied Aaron, he noticed her left eye was a baby-blue color, and her right eye was a beautiful cream color.

Another gargoyle creature landed close by. The angelic being turned and began to fight. As this was happening, Aaron saw more disgusting, diseased bodies slipping through the glimmering wall. They would fall to the ground where the black lizard creatures would descend upon them. As they ate the bodies, the mouths of these people would scream in terror. It seemed to Aaron, these people had died, yet they were somewhat aware of their hell-like situations, at least until the creatures had finished with them.

At the same time, there would be brilliant bolts of light from the wall. Some were close to Aaron, and others appeared to be miles away. These light bolts would streak across the sky, never dropping into the blackness of the ground.

While the angel and the gargoyle fought, another angel landed and then another. Soon, another gargoyle landed and began attacking the angelic beings.

Once the first angel had struck down the gargoyle she was fighting, she turned to Aaron. Again, he was captivated by her eyes. She paid no attention to this, and with her free hand, she reached inside his upper body, penetrating the very flesh itself. He was shocked and frightened as he looked down to see her hand inside his upper body. He could feel it as well, yet there was no pain.

After doing something inside his upper body, the angel extracted her hand, took hold of him, and pulled him away from the wall. He was horrified to see there was only half of him in her arms as she took flight.

As she flew from the wall, Aaron noticed a thin thread streaming from his body, very similar to what he saw when the medics carried his body away on the other side of the wall. He could also feel a strange sensation inside but could think of no words to describe the feeling.

As the angel flew swiftly, carrying him over the black, evil-looking creatures on the ground, he felt a horror and dark, empty sadness that was as he had never felt. Then, more gargoyles swooped in close and began attacking the angel as she carried him.

He looked back and saw other angels were fighting the gargoyles as they tried to get to him as well as the thin thread streaming from him.

Suddenly, Aaron began to cry. He sensed the evil that lay below him and the danger his very being was now in, and it became completely overwhelming. Tears streamed down his face as if he were a small child.

Again, and again, the evil gargoyle creatures would attack, appearing very desperate to take Aaron from the angelic woman. Again, and again, angels would repel the creatures.

Through tear-soaked eyes, Aaron could see more and more angels and gargoyles also fighting all around the thin thread streaming from his half body. The battle stretched back for what looked to be miles. It seemed to be a frenzied fight by the gargoyles to take Aaron or take hold of the thread streaming from his being.

All along this thread, the struggle was intensifying as more and more angels, as well as gargoyles, joined in. Aaron could not imagine what would happen to him if the gargoyles reached the thread.

Then, unexpectedly, he and the angel carrying him entered a bright area of light. When this happened, the thin thread instantly became light as well. When the thread became illuminated, the angels stopped fighting and let the gargoyles fly to it. Several of the evil beings tried to stop themselves but could not turn back fast enough. As the creatures flew into the thread, they were sliced in two, as if the thread had become a brilliant razor.

After viewing this, Aaron lost awareness.

When he woke, Aaron found himself sitting in a chair. Raising his head, he saw the recreation room at his barracks in Fort Hood, Texas.

Aaron looked around, and there was no one to be seen. The television in front of him was turned on, but it had a black and white, snowy screen and white noise.

For several seconds, Aaron examined his surroundings. Although he was familiar with this place, it was apparent there was something very different. The light was all around, yet there seemed to be no source. Looking up, he noticed there were no light fixtures in the ceiling.

As he looked back down, a man was sitting in the chair across from him and to the right of the TV. Aaron was astounded that he didn't jump from the shock of someone suddenly being where there was no one before. But, oddly, he wasn't afraid at all.

The man wore army fatigues, and Aaron noticed he had the rank of captain.

Standing quickly, Aaron came to attention and saluted the officer.

"At ease," the captain said, with a low, authoritative voice that sounded almost as if it were coming from an amplifier.

Aaron changed his stance to "at ease."

"Please, sit down, soldier," the captain said.

Aaron sat back down.

For several seconds, the two simply looked at each other. Then Aaron spoke.

"Sir, I'm confused. I don't understand how I got here. Have I lost my memory, or what?"

"Well, what do you remember?" the officer asked.

"I was in Vietnam. We were attacked by the Vietcong. Huey helicopters came, and we were bugging out. I was sort of in one, but not all the way. The pilot was hit, and the chopper tilted. I fell out. It must have been forty or fifty feet from the ground. Then, when I hit..."

Aaron stopped as the very strange memories came back to him. The captain studied him.

"Then what?" the captain asked.

Aaron looked around again. He sensed for certain now that he wasn't at Fort Hood. But it looked so real.

"Then, some very strange memories. I don't know. Maybe I was dreaming."

"You weren't dreaming."

Aaron looked at the captain. Again, he felt that he should be shocked. But he still felt calm.

"When our guardians found you, the death wraiths were very close to taking you. Fortunately, they were able to get you here. Otherwise, you might have found yourself in the depths of the underworld, where the remainder of your soul would have been sucked dry by the dwellers of that unspeakable region."

Once again, Aaron felt oddly calm upon hearing this horrific possibility.

"I don't, uhm… Where am I, sir?"

"You're in an area that is between the physical world and, well, another realm of existence that we call the second realm. It could be described as a very small, isolated area on the edge of the spiritual realm, perhaps like a small island."

Aaron strained at the idea. "Do you mean purgatory?"

"Well, it is likely what some have described as purgatory. But it's not the purgatory that many have written of. Though it certainly may have been identified as such.

"You're in a place that is necessary for the balance of interactions between the physical and spiritual realms."

After some thought, Aaron replied. "I didn't know there was a place in the spiritual realm that looked like Fort Hood."

The captain smiled. "Actually, it looks like a place that your mind can understand and relate to. For someone else, it would look completely different. Your mind devised this 'spiritual Fort Hood' for you to relate to and understand what the mind cannot really comprehend."

Once again, Aaron considered the information. Finally, after a few seconds of thought, he asked, "How did I get here? I mean, why am I here? Am I alive or dead?"

"You're what might be called both alive and dead. In the physical world, you're in a comatose state. Here, you're alive and well, but in an environment that is not hospitable to your physical being.

"As to why and how you got here, you are undoubtedly what would be called a 'unique case,' an anomaly, if you will. It's not uncommon for people to find their way here. But they do so in a spiritual sense. It often takes years of training to enter this realm. When done so by the spiritual method, these people move across the sphere of death as if they were vapor. Their presence is not perceived by the gatekeepers of the dead.

"However, you entered the realm in a rare manner. Your spirit, or soul, left your body at the instant of what would have been death. So, what happened is you didn't die, but you didn't live either. Thus, you're here."

Aaron's eyes squinted as he considered this.

"So, what happens now?"

"That's a good question. Much of what happens now is up to you," the captain replied.

"How is it up to me? I don't understand." Aaron shook his head in disbelief. "I don't understand any of this."

"The fact that you are here now means you do have the ability to understand. Not only can you understand, but you can utilize the information here as well as in the physical world. Due to your unique situation, you have potential far beyond the others who come here for training and wisdom."

After saying this, the captain stood and walked over to the pool table. He picked up a pool stick and began shooting balls into the pockets.

Aaron stood and walked over to the table. He watched the captain for a few seconds, then asked him, "How do I understand this, and how do I change it?"

The captain looked at him and asked, "Until you understand it, how do you know if you want to change it?"

Aaron thought about this as the captain shot another ball into the corner pocket. Then, seeming to sense Aaron was struggling, he laid the pool cue on the table.

"You were fighting in a war when you crossed the plane of existence. You should now sense there is another war, a war that has been raging since the dawn of time, a war that mankind is involved with, though only on a small scale. For the most part, mankind is still the equivalent of a spiritual child, perhaps, like a teenager. They think they've got it all figured out and know so much, but this is, in fact, the very attitude that keeps them from seeing more, from growing beyond the barriers they face."

Suddenly, Aaron's days in Sunday school and church service began to come back.

"The war between God and Satan," he said, almost to himself.

"Yes, you know about the war," the captain said.

"I heard the stories in Sunday school. I remember sermons our pastor gave. But they all seemed like ancient history. I believed them, but it seemed to be long ago and far away."

The captain walked over to the window. He glanced out and then turned to Aaron.

"It's a war that has been going on long before the earth or mankind was around. Your world is affected less than other worlds. Yet, the enemy would bring total darkness and death to all if it were ever victorious.

"Now, you must make a decision. You must decide if you will fight for good or return to your world and allow natural laws to take their course.

"Or, there is one other option; death."

Aaron walked over to the window next to the captain. Looking out, he saw a small squad of soldiers doing exercises.

"Who are they?" Aaron asked.

"They're soldiers of light. Few can make it here. Fewer still can endure the training needed to be functional in the physical world. Those are the few that have made it past the initial trials. Their training will begin soon."

There were eleven soldiers in a small parade area. Soon, they were called into formation, and what appeared to be a sergeant inspected them and dismissed the group.

"Are they like me?" Aaron asked.

"No, not entirely. They've reached this place through meditation. They're here spiritually, but their bodies are in the physical realm. They've not crossed the valley of the dead in the same manner as you are."

"So, if I choose to let nature run its course, what will happen?" Aaron asked.

"I don't know. You'll be returned, and depending on your ability to recover, you will live or die. The laws of nature follow their own path. It's the way the creator intended, and regardless of what some may say, it's a sufficient system."

"And, if I choose to fight for good, what does that mean?" Aaron asked.

"It means you will choose the most difficult path. You will endure extensive training here. Then, the real trials will start when you return to the physical realm. The life of a soldier of light is not an easy one. You will encounter and combat evil that most men don't understand or even believe exists. There will be few in the physical realm that can assist you in your battles. However, you will have an understanding that what you're doing is of a higher good, much nobler than the war you were fighting in the physical sense."

Aaron walked over and sat back down, expelling a long breath of air.

"I'm no hero—not like that."

The captain also sat down across from him.

"Actually, you are who you are. Deep down, you know who you are. And if you were not that kind of hero, you would not be here. You chose something other than dying. You chose to find a place that you could be who you are. You've known for some time now that you were different.

36

What you must do now is either accept who you are or lose faith in something you've felt for a long time."

When the captain said this, Aaron suddenly saw the truth. It was there all along. He had always known it deep in his soul.

The sudden revelation caused a tear to erupt from Aaron's eye. He asked, "What must I do?"

"You know that as well. Before you can do anything else, you must repent and be cleansed."

Aaron immediately fell to his knees and repented. As he arose, he became a complete person. He knew who he was and what the creator had intended him to be.

"Get some rest," the captain then said. Aaron went to his room. It was just as he recalled from Fort Hood. Everything was the same, except he had no roommate. He climbed into his bunk, and sleep quickly overcame him.

CHAPTER THREE:

Nirvana

The following morning, a knock came on the door.

"First call! First call!"

Aaron climbed out of his bunk and opened the door. There was no one there.

He opened his locker and found it to be fully stocked with fatigues, dress uniforms and several sets of civilian clothing.

After getting dressed, he made his way to the parade grounds. There, he fell into formation with eleven other soldiers.

As he looked at the others, he realized their faces were not clear or distinctive. The other soldiers seemed to be made up of a mist-like substance rather than flesh. He glanced down at his hand to reassure himself that he saw flesh.

After a burly sergeant, who was as Aaron, made of flesh, came and inspected the twelve soldiers, they were dismissed. Aaron went to the mess hall and ate, completely alone. Just as his locker and room, the mess hall was fully furnished with food and everything needed to eat. Yet, there was no one there.

After breakfast, Aaron went back toward the barracks. Looking across the area, he could see other soldiers in the distance. They also were not clear or distinctive, so he felt they too must have traveled across the valley of death by meditation.

As he approached his barracks, the sergeant seemed to appear from nowhere and met him at the steps.

"Your first class is 'Fundamental Planes of Existence.' It will be in the building to the back of the barracks, room 221. The instructor will direct you to your next class afterwards."

"Yes, Sergeant," Aaron replied and made his way to the building next door.

Thus, began his training in all matters of the spiritual realm and interactions of the physical world. Time seemed to stand still, though he did have an awareness of it.

What felt like several weeks after his arrival, the sergeant came to his class.

"You're needed in the recreation room," he said and then left.

Aaron stood up and, after nodding to the instructor, who also appeared like a thick mist, left and went to the recreation room.

Walking into the large open bay, Aaron noticed the television was on, and it had what first appeared to be a program playing.

On closer examination, he was startled to see Ping. She was looking at the screen and crying. Then Aaron saw Anderson move into the picture behind her.

"Spyder, you hear me, sweeheart?" Ping said as tears rolled down her cheeks.

Aaron suddenly realized she was looking at his physical body.

"Spyder, you hear me? Please wake up."

"He can't hear anything, Ping. I don't know that he's even in there anymore," Anderson told her with a look of compassion.

"What's going happen to him?" Ping asked as she wiped tears from her eyes.

"If he doesn't wake up soon, they'll ship him back to the states. His parents will decide on pulling the plug or not."

When Anderson said this, Ping turned to him with fear in her eyes.

"Pull plug? What you mean, pull plug?"

"Take him off life support," Anderson replied.

"You mean kill him? Why? No, they must not do so!"

"It's not up to us, Ping. It's a decision his parents will have to make. But maybe he'll come out of it."

The television then faded to the usual snowy picture.

Aaron noticed the captain was sitting across from him and immediately stood and came to attention.

"At ease. Please sit," the captain said.

Aaron sat back down. "Seems I'm in pretty bad shape, sir."

The captain smiled, "The spirit is much stronger than the flesh. You'll be all right. But it's good for you to know what's happening in the physical realm. There will soon come a time that you must reach across the divide. Your next class should help. It deals with transcendental dynamics."

"Yes, sir," Aaron replied, and the captain dismissed him.

For what seemed like months, Aaron trained. On another occasion, he went to the recreation room and watched as his physical body was being taken aboard an airplane. It was a strange sensation to view the medical personnel hooking up the life support that was necessary to keep him alive. He watched a while longer as the plane took off and the tubes and oxygen lines swayed about, but then he lost interest and went back to his room for some rest.

Not long after viewing the plane ride, Aaron was again called from a training session. As he stood along with his fellow soldiers in a semicircle around the instructor, the sergeant walked up and informed him he was needed in the recreation room.

When Aaron entered the room, he was met with the image of his mother on the television screen. She was looking at him and crying.

"Aaron, son." She then wiped her eyes with a handkerchief.

As he sat down and studied his mother's face, the captain appeared in a chair across from him and spoke, "This is an extremely critical time. You must reach across the divide if you are to survive."

Aaron glanced at the captain and then turned back to the television screen.

"Is there any hope that he'll wake up?" his mother asked a doctor, who now came into view.

"There's always a slight hope. But your son has been in a coma for months now. The odds are against him ever waking up."

As the doctor said this, Aaron saw his father move over beside his mother. He could see the stress on his father's face as he examined his son, lying on the hospital bed in a coma.

"Perhaps it would be better if we… let him go, Ruth."

When his father said this, Aaron's mother turned to him, "What, just let him die? What are you saying, Jess? He's our son."

"I know, but he may be in pain. We just don't know."

His mother replied quickly with fear in her voice, "You heard the doctor. He said there's always a little hope."

"And he also said the odds are against Aaron ever waking up. What if he's suffering right now?"

Aaron leaned over, his arms resting on his knees. He studied the situation carefully.

His father turned to the doctor and began talking with him. His mother examined Aaron's face; she was still crying.

As she was stroking his hair, she spoke softly.

"Aaron, son, are you still there? Please let us know."

His mother then took Aaron's hand in hers. At this instant, Aaron focused his mind. He took his own hands and clasped them together. Closing his eyes, he gently squeezed them.

His mother almost screamed, "Jess!! Jess! He, he squeezed my hand! He's still there, Jess!"

"What, what are you talking about?" his father asked, turning from the doctor.

"I asked him if he was still with us. I asked him to let us know! He squeezed my hand. He let me know. We can't let him die, Jess. He's still with us!"

Aaron glanced over to the captain; he smiled and nodded to Aaron.

His mother and father talked for a while longer but decided they would not pull the plug on their son. He would stay in a Fort Leavenworth hospital, which was several hundred miles from Aaron's home near Hays, Kansas. They told the doctor they would visit regularly and perhaps someday in the future make the decision. But for now, his mother would not allow him to die.

****

Aaron's training continued, but from time to time, he would visit the recreation room and observe his mother or sister visit his physical body. On one occasion, he sat and listened while his father talked about events back at their family ranch. Then his father wiped a tear from his eye as he looked at his son.

Finally, the day of his graduation came. It was a simple ceremony. The captain pinned several pins upon his uniform, which indicated Aaron's abilities in the physical realm.

Afterwards, the captain called Aaron into his office.

"Have a seat, please." The captain motioned to a chair in front of his desk, and Aaron sat down. "You've completed your training, but you can still fail to even begin your assigned task."

"How so, sir?" Aaron asked.

"When you return to your physical body and wake up, the memory of this place will be clear and fresh. However, if you don't act on the training and experiences of this place, the memories and training will begin to fade. You will begin to believe it was only a dream. The longer it takes for you to act upon your objective, the more the training and memories will seem to be… unreal. Your mind will begin to reason it was all a dream."

Aaron considered this, "I understand, sir."

"Good. As you're aware, Uriel, the angel of light, has agreed to aid you. Use his assistance sparingly in the physical realm."

"Yes, sir," Aaron replied.

The captain continued, "Your primary task is one known as 'The Defiler.'"

Aaron studied the captain. It seemed he was expected to speak.

"Yes, sir. How will I locate my primary task?"

"You'll travel to the Crescent City, which is tethered to a ribbon. From there, you will locate a trail of death. Beware. The Defiler is a formidable foe."

Again, silence held the room. Then Aaron asked, "How do I find the trail of death?"

The captain continued, as if waiting for Aaron's question, "You must do three things. Never turn down a gift or invitation. The gifts are often sent from your support team in the second realm. Invitations are often doors opened to lead you to the next path or doorway. Finally, never refuse a favor or offer of help. Favors are often inspired to aid you in your mission.

"As for identifying the path, you'll know a death carrier after you first see one. Your spiritual perception will naturally increase as you realign yourself with your task.

"When the death carrier is close to triggering, you'll know you've located the trail. However, you can't intervene with death carriers, unless it's to protect yourself.

"Once a death carrier is identified, follow its trail, and you will eventually locate The Defiler, or... perish along the way."

Aaron grimaced a bit but quickly recovered. A few seconds later, he replied, "Yes, sir. Thank you, sir."

That evening, the sergeant knocked on Aaron's door.

"Hello, Sergeant," Aaron said after opening the door.

"I came to wish you luck and Godspeed. Are you ready?"

"Thank you, Sergeant. I feel that I am ready," Aaron replied.

"Good. Then I'm also here to inform you that when you wake, you'll have crossed the plane of existence. You'll awake in the physical realm. Try not to be too shocked; it could result in injury. Also, your physical body has degraded some during your time here. You'll need to recover before beginning your mission. But it's imperative that you keep the mission in your thoughts, or you will begin to lose the training and knowledge. Once you locate the path to your primary task, all your training and studies from here will begin to return and grow stronger."

Aaron nodded. The weathered-looking sergeant nodded as well. He reached out his hand and Aaron shook it. The sergeant turned and left.

As the light faded, Aaron lay down in his bunk. He was nervous. His heart beat rapidly. Finally, after what seemed hours, he drifted off to sleep.

CHAPTER FOUR:

Resurrection

With a painful sensation and a feeling of being shocked by electricity, Aaron sat up in bed. Immediately, the feeding hose in his mouth and running down his throat began to choke him. He reached up and began desperately pulling the tubes and attachments from his face. He fell from the bed. A loud crashing sound echoed through the large bay room as IV-holding devices and other articles related to keeping him alive hit the floor.

As he was pulling the attachments and tubes from his face, nurses ran in.

"Oh my God! Oh my God!! Call the doctor, quickly!" A nurse shouted to another.

"It's all right, dear!! Calm down, please, calm down, it's all right! Oh my God, I can't believe you're awake. It's okay, hon, please calm down!"

As the nurse attempted to calm Aaron, he finally removed the feeding tube from his throat and, after coughing for several seconds, took in a deep breath.

"Please just sit still, dear. Oh… my God, I can't believe this!" the nurse exclaimed again, then turning to the door shouted, "Can someone please get a doctor in here?"

Several hours later, Aaron sat propped up in his bed as the doctor finished examining him.

"You've dodged a bullet somehow, Mr. Prescott. It's very seldom a person wakes up after so many months in a coma. I'm thrilled that you did. It gives us some hope here on this ward. We've not had a patient wake up in years. So, thank you for that."

Aaron was in a daze. His mind felt foggy and almost everything hurt. He felt weak and moving any part of his body was difficult to do.

Looking at the doctor, he nodded. His throat was still irritated from the tubes. It was difficult to swallow and even more difficult to talk.

He was moved from the coma ward and the next morning woke to find his mother, father and sister in the room.

"Oh, my dear lord, Aaron," his mother sighed, embracing him. He struggled to wake up as his father and sister stood behind his mother, smiling.

It was several days before his mind was clear enough to notice his condition. He had lost weight. His muscles had deteriorated, and it took great effort to do anything, after which he was winded and needed to relax and catch his breath.

His mother stayed at the hospital as Aaron began to recover. Two weeks later, he was moved to a rehabilitation center.

As he worked to regain his strength, his mind went over the events he recalled during his time in a coma. Even after he could speak, he talked very little. His mother was obviously concerned as this was not the son she remembered. Yet, Aaron could only think of his experiences from the second realm. Doubt entered his mind often. He struggled to hold onto the reality of what he had endured. He began to focus on what he had gone through. He decided he must prove it was either real or not. He must recover and find the truth.

Six weeks later, Aaron sat in front of a desk. The doctor behind the desk examined the paperwork in front of him.

"Mr. Prescott, you've recovered fairly well in a short time, but you have a long way to go. I do feel you've recovered enough to go home. You'll need to continue the physical therapy at the designated facility in Hays."

The doctor glanced up at Aaron. He adjusted his glasses and continued, "You've been given a full medical discharge. Although there's no single reason for this type of discharge, it's been concluded that your body endured a massive and traumatic experience due to the fall from the helicopter in Vietnam. The recommendation is for you to resist hard labor or situations that will cause stress or exertion to your body. We can't say for certain, but there could very well be unseen nerve damage. So, try to limit your activities. Perhaps you could write or try artwork. There are plenty of low-stress opportunities if you look for them."

Aaron nodded.

"All right, unless you have any questions, I'll sign you out of here, and you can go home."

"Thank you, doctor," Aaron replied, and the doctor signed the paperwork.

On the way home, Aaron opened the window and let the summer breeze flow through his hair. His mother glanced back to him and smiled. He smiled back, though it felt almost fake.

The family ranch had not changed much as they pulled down the long drive. Six hundred and fifty acres of farm and ranch land. When he'd left for his second tour in Vietnam, there were five hundred and seventy head of cattle, give or take a few. And hundreds of acres in wheat, corn and maize.

The large two-story house finally came into view. Once they were stopped, Aaron got out and examined the only real home he had ever known.

Using a cane to make sure he didn't fall; he made his way up the front porch. His mother walked beside him but seemed to sense he would want to get up the steps by himself, so she refrained from helping him.

Over the next week, his sister, brother-in-law and nephew came and stayed a few days. Aunts and uncles came and went as well. His grandparents on both sides of the family visited for several days each before returning home.

After the third week, Aaron began walking around without a cane. But now, his memories of the realm beyond the valley of death were fading. He began to feel anxious and concerned.

"Have you ever heard of a 'Crescent City,' Dad?"

Aaron's father glanced up from his food. He wiped his mouth with a napkin, "Can't say that I have. Is it supposed to be in Kansas?"

Aaron used his fork to move a piece of steak around on his plate.

"I'm not sure. It could be just about anywhere, I suppose," Aaron replied, never turning from his dinner.

"Hmm, I don't think it's in Kansas, or I would have heard of it, unless it's just one of those tiny towns out east. But it would be odd to name it Crescent City if it were just a little town. Why do you ask, son?"

Glancing up from his plate, he replied, "Oh, no reason. I just heard it somewhere."

The following morning, Aaron went to the old barn out behind his house. Opening the doors, he saw what he had come to find.

Walking over to a dust tarp, he reached up and pulled it from his 1965 Plymouth Belvedere II. He had put it up on blocks and prepared it for storage before he went back to Vietnam. He looked over the jet-black car. He had done most of the work on it himself. Many of the modifications took place in the barn where his car now sat in storage; though he did have a friend in Hays repaint the car.

"You about ready to get her out on the road?"

Aaron turned to see his dad standing in the open doors.

"Yeah, I think so."

"I'll help you get her going again," his dad replied.

An hour later, the Plymouth was running, and Aaron pulled it out of the barn.

Aaron's dad walked up to the driver's side window.

"I think I'll take it to town, get it filled up with gas," Aaron said as his dad cleaned a tool with a grease rag.

"All right. You going to be back for dinner?"

"Oh, I might just grab something in Hays. Thanks for the help, Dad." Aaron then gave his father a quick smile, put the car in gear and drove down the long driveway.

Later, he found himself at the Hays public library. Sitting at a large desk, he thumbed through atlases and books on population and geography.

After an hour and a half, a stack of hardback reference books sat on his right side. He expelled a breath of frustration as a library worker pushed a rolling cart full of books by.

The elderly man stopped.

"Long day?" he asked with a hushed voice.

"Not so much long as unproductive," Aaron replied.

"What book are you looking for? Maybe I can help."

"Well, thanks but I'm not looking for a book. I'm looking for someplace called Crescent City... and one that's 'tethered to a ribbon,' if it even exists."

The library worker perked up.

"Oh, you're looking for New Orleans then."

"What?" Aaron looked up at the elderly man.

"New Orleans, you know, the Crescent City. It's shaped like a crescent. My father was from that area. He called it the Crescent City all the time. Not many people call it that now though."

Aaron continued to study the man with curiosity.

"What about the 'ribbon' thing?"

The man scratched his chin, "My guess would be it's tethered to a ribbon of water. That being the Mississippi river. Just a guess though."

Before Aaron could reply, the man continued, "It's interesting to me that you were given the information in riddle form. To my understanding, information in such a format is retained by the brain longer than an ordinary name, which can become confused with similar names and places."

Aaron continued to stare at the man with an impressed silence. Finally, he replied, "Thank you, sir. Thank you very much."

The man smiled, nodded and, pushing his cart, walked away.

The following day, after breakfast, Aaron began to pack. His mother walked past his open bedroom door, then stopped and moved back.

Looking in, she watched as Aaron placed folded clothes in a duffle bag. He glanced at his mother as she examined the bass guitar case and small amplifier by the door. Then she looked at the suitcase on the bed as her son placed another shirt in the duffle bag.

Finally, his mother asked, "Are you… going somewhere?"

Aaron's face twisted slightly as he glanced at his mother. He grabbed several pair of socks from an open dresser drawer and then replied, "Yeah, I'm, uhh, I'm going somewhere."

His mother's face dropped a bit. "Oh, I see. Are you sure you're ready? You may want to recover a bit more. It seems a little soon to be leaving."

He placed the socks in the duffle bag and then began to close it up.

"I need to go, Mom. I'm doing great, feeling good. I think the traveling will help me."

"Oh, I see… Well, your father will want to see you before you go. Are you going to be gone long?"

Aaron stopped what he was doing. He looked at her, and his mouth twisted a little, "Yeah, uhm, I was planning to tell Dad bye. I, well, I'm not sure how long I'll be gone. I'll call."

He could see her eyes tearing up. She nodded and smiled, then left the doorway, in an effort it seemed to hide the tears from her son.

Aaron drove an old farm truck out to the field where his father was working with several hired ranch hands. When his father saw him, he walked over to the truck.

"Hey, you bring lunch out?" his dad asked.

"Uhmm, no, sorry. How's it going?" Aaron asked as he climbed out of the truck.

"Oh, fairly well, we're just reworking the fence in this section." His dad then straightened up and studied Aaron, seeming to sense something.

"Well, I, mmm, I just came out to say good-bye, Dad. I'm packed up, and I'm going to be leaving shortly."

His dad studied Aaron briefly. He took a deep breath in, nodded and exhaled.

"This is a bit sudden, son. You should probably heal up some more."

"Yeah, I'm sorry I didn't give more warning. I just need to get away and do some things. To resolve some things in my mind."

Again, his dad nodded.

"Does your mother know?"

"Yeah, I told her earlier."

For several seconds Jess examined his son, then asked. "So, where you off to?"

"New Orleans."

Jess's face expressed a bit of surprise.

"Aaron, I know you must have gone through a lot over there. I sense you've changed from your experiences in Vietnam. I understand there may be things you need to work out, but, there's a lot of room in Kansas. Don't you think you could work these things out a little closer to home?"

Aaron expressed discomfort, "Well, I really need to go a little farther away, Dad. I'm sorry, it's just kind of difficult to explain."

Once again, his father studied him. For several long seconds only the sound of the hired hands working on the fence was heard. Finally, his dad replied, "All right, son. I trust your judgment. You'll call, won't you?"

"Yeah, I'll call when I get there."

His father shook his hand, then he hugged Aaron.

"Thanks, Dad."

Aaron smiled, turned and went back to the old farm truck. It started with a puff of smoke, and he was soon headed slowly back across the rough field.

Later, Aaron stopped by the bank in Hays. He had deposited his many months of army pay received during his time in a coma, as well as pay he had received monthly for his medical discharge status. After taking out half his money and then placing another quarter of his funds into cashier's checks, he began his trip to Louisiana.

54

CHAPTER FIVE:

Mostly Cloudy with a Chance for Sunny

Almost a week after leaving Hays, Aaron was pulling into the outskirts of New Orleans.

Watching out the window, he drove slowly. He wondered what he should do and, on several occasions, thought he might be a little crazy for driving so far to begin with.

For twenty minutes he crept along street after street. The sun was lowering onto the horizon, and he considered looking for a motel.

Then he spotted something. He slowed and pulled into a gas station with a large, faded sign reading "Crescent City Service Station."

Realizing he could use some gas in the Plymouth, he moved up to the pump. A service attendant approached as Aaron got out of the car.

"Fill her up and check the oil," Aaron said. Then asked, "Where's your restroom?"

"Over on the other side of the station," the attendant replied as he started opening the hood.

Aaron went to the bathroom. He stepped back out a few minutes later and looked around. Still he saw nothing to give him any direction.

Walking back toward his car, he passed a large maroon sedan parked in front of the station.

He moved over to the Plymouth as the service attendant was closing the hood.

"Oil's level, sir."

"Okay, thanks," Aaron replied. He then stood by his car as the man finished filling the tank.

From the front of the station, a man walked out the door with a pack of cigarettes in his hand. He climbed into the sedan, and the car started.

Examining the car, a little closer, he noticed the windows were rolled halfway down. He could see a young woman in the front passenger seat and another in the back seat. Aaron then turned back to the attendant who now approached him.

"That'll be four dollars and fifteen cents."

Aaron nodded and handed the man a five-dollar bill.

"I'll be right back with your change, sir." The attendant then raced off toward the station.

The front passenger side window of the sedan rolled all the way down, and a young woman popped her head out.

"Hey, you want to go to a party?"

Aaron smiled a little smile and then said, "I'm kind of busy right now, but thanks."

The woman then turned to the back seat, "Roll your window down," she said.

"What?" The young woman in the back seat asked.

"Just do it!" The woman in the front seat replied.

The back window began to roll down, and Aaron saw a very attractive young woman with long blonde hair. She quickly gave him a quirky, uninterested smile.

"Hey, she's the one that asked if you wanted to go to a party. Are you going to turn down an invitation from her?"

The attendant walked back up to Aaron. "Here's your change, sir."

"What did you say?" Aaron asked.

"I said here's your change."

"Not you, her."

The young woman gave him an odd expression.

"I said she invited you to a party. Are you really going to turn her down?"

Aaron looked at the young woman again. She smiled once more but then began to roll the window back up.

"No, I'm not going to turn her invitation down," Aaron said.

"Great, just follow us," the woman in the front seat replied. The car began to back out as Aaron moved quickly around to the driver's side of his car.

"Uhm, your change, sir?"

"Keep it," Aaron said as he jumped into his car and, starting it, quickly pulled away to catch up to the large sedan.

Following close behind, he saw the blonde woman and the one in the front passenger seat waving back to him. He smiled a little and waved to them.

The two cars drove about three miles until they came to an area where the houses thinned out and woodlands became more prevalent.

A few miles more and Aaron could see a large fire burning in a vacant field. Cars, trucks and a few motorcycles were parked around the fire.

As they maneuvered through the vehicles, he could hear rock and roll blaring from a van that had the doors opened.

Aaron parked behind the sedan. Soon the woman in front jumped out. The man who had bought the cigarettes at the station also got out from the driver's side.

"Woooowweee!!!" the young brunette shouted and began to dance about. The driver, who appeared to be twenty-five, walked back toward Aaron. He had long hair and a beard. He also wore bell bottom pants and a buckskin vest with frills.

"Righteous ride, dude. Did you do the work?"

Aaron glanced at the Plymouth as the man bent over to admire the chrome rims.

"Most of it. I didn't do the paint job."

"I bet it'll book ass!"

The young brunette woman danced up to them. "Someone needs to powder her nose, but she'll be right out!"

The woman pointed to the back of the sedan as she continued to dance around.

Aaron smiled slightly, nodded and then began to look around.

"Oh, there's Ronnie! Hey Ronnie!" The brunette woman took off, and the man that drove the sedan followed behind her.

As he examined his surroundings, Aaron quickly spotted something that captured his full attention. Directly across from him, standing around the van with the music playing, were several people. A large, burly man was turning up a bottle of booze. A thin, sickly-looking man was smoking something, which he then passed to several other men and women. But there was one man among the group that Aaron examined very closely.

The man that had caught Aaron's interest had a strange red glow around his face. Aaron focused on the man and realized his face had what appeared to be a glowing red skull image. He was drinking a beer and talking to a young woman, but the red skull image was clear and not something Aaron had ever seen in his life.

Looking at the van he saw a sign painted on the side that read 'Lefevere Brothers Garage.'

"Hi, I'm Sonya."

Aaron glanced over and saw the pretty blonde woman standing beside him with her hand out to shake. She wore a lacy top and bell bottom pants.

He nodded and then turned back to the man with the odd glow around his face.

"Who's that?" Aaron asked, never turning back to Sonya.

Sonya gave Aaron a strange look and lowered her hand as she glanced over to the van.

"That's the Lefevere brothers. They're slime. Actually... slime rates a little higher in my opinion. Why?"

"Do they live around here?" Aaron asked.

Again, Sonya looked at Aaron as if he were a little off in the head.

"Uhm, yeah, they have a garage on Jackson Street."

As she said this, the brunette and the man with her came back toward them.

"Did you get your powdering done, Sunny?" the brunette asked.

"Who's that man? The one with the black shirt?" Aaron asked, still not turning to Sonya.

"Uhmmm, I don't know. Probably a slimeball mechanic for the brothers. They're all real strange. And, speaking of which!"

Aaron looked at Sonya, and she was giving him a very odd expression. The brunette and man came closer. Aaron looked at the three.

"Someone is going to die here very soon. If you don't want to witness it, you should leave now."

Aaron then moved toward his car.

"What? Really? You're a real weirdo, you know that!" Sonya almost shouted as he opened the door of the Plymouth.

"You sure know how to pick 'em, Sunny," the brunette said loudly as Aaron started the car.

As the sun was setting and Aaron pulled away from the party, he heard Sonya shout, "JERK!"

When Aaron got back to the city, he found Jackson Street. He didn't have to go far before spotting the Lefevere brother's garage.

He then went back to the Crescent City Service Station and bought a newspaper from a stand outside. He pulled over to a parking lot that had a large streetlight.

Sitting on the hood of his car, he began looking through the newspaper.

Shortly after this, a police car drove down the street with its siren blaring. Aaron glanced up as it passed by.

A few minutes later, an ambulance came down the street with lights and siren at full blast. It headed in the direction of the party. Aaron again glanced up but quickly returned his attention to the newspaper.

Twenty minutes later, as he studied the classified section for rental houses, the large maroon sedan drove by. It slowed down, and Sonya scooted over, then rolled the window down. Her eyes were swollen from crying. She stared at Aaron as the car almost came to a stop but then crept on past. He never looked up from the newspaper.

Later, Aaron rented a room at a motel. He got cleaned up and went to bed.

The following morning, he began searching for a house close to the area. All day he called from pay phones and then went and looked at rental properties.

That afternoon he sat at a drive-in burger place, which was not far from Jackson Street. It had been a fruitless day of searching for a place to live. The windows were rolled down, and the humid heat drifted through the car as he ate a hamburger and again glanced over the classifieds.

Suddenly, the passenger door opened. Sonya climbed into the car and then shut the door back. Her long blonde hair was in a ponytail. She wore a tight, frilly top that showed her belly button and snug fitting bell bottom jeans. She smiled at Aaron as he looked at her with a surprised and puzzled expression.

"Hi," she said and waved with her fingers.

Aaron had stopped chewing his food due to the shock of someone unexpectedly getting into his car. But he again chewed and nodded a little. Sonya simply continued to smile and stare at him. Finally, he swallowed his food.

"Can I help you?" he asked, appearing very confused.

"Yeah, you can tell me how you knew that guy you were talking about last night was going to kill someone. He got into a fight not long after you left. He pulled out a gun and shot the man he was fighting. How did you know that was going to happen?"

Aaron picked up his soda and took a drink, still watching Sonya.

"Intuition?" he finally said, then took another bite of his hamburger.

"Intuition? For real?" Her face expressed disbelief. "That's one hell of an intuition!" she replied.

Aaron chewed his food but continued to glance at her. After he finished his bite, he asked, "Are you... here with someone, or...?"

"No, I was with Judy and Paul. You met them last night. But we saw your car and I had them drop me off."

Aaron nodded a little and sat his half-eaten burger on the console, then wiped his mouth with a napkin.

"So, what's your name?" she asked.

Aaron looked around, as if hoping her friends would show back up and take her away. When he concluded this was not going to happen, he turned his attention back to her.

"Well, my friends call me Spyder."

Sonya almost laughed and blurted out, "Spyder? No lie? Spyder?"

Aaron nodded and said, "Yeah, but my name is Aaron. You can call me Aaron if you want."

"Are you kidding? Spyder is sooo fab! It's way groovier than Aaron."

She smiled brightly and then asked, "You got something to drink?"

Aaron glanced around. He picked up his soda. "This is all I've..."

Before he could finish, she took it from his hand and began drinking it. Then, still holding the straw in her fingers, said, "Thanks, I was parched."

Aaron nodded, expressing dismay.

"So, Spyder, I've decided I'm going to do you a favor and help you."

Aaron's eyes widened. "Help me with what?"

"Help you find a place. What did you think?"

"What makes you think I'm looking for a place?"

She smiled slyly, "You're not the only one with 'intuition'."

Sonya then pointed at the hamburger. "You gonna eat that?"

Aaron glanced at the half-eaten burger on the console. "Uhmm, no, I guess not."

She picked it up and took a bite.

"Uh, what's your name, by the way?" he asked.

Sonya turned and looked at him with anger-filled eyes. She chewed her bite and then replied with her mouth half-full, "You don't remember my name?"

"I'm sorry, but no, I don't."

She appeared to swell up a little. Then finished chewing and swallowed her bite.

"You know, Spyder, when a beautiful girl tells a guy her name, most guys remember the name."

Aaron leaned back against the door; his face twisted again with apprehension over the entire situation. He inhaled as Sonya took another bite of his hamburger.

"Well, this is just a little unusual for me. I'm sorry."

She smiled as she tried to finish her bite, then replied, with a little less mouthful this time.

"It's all right. I forgive you." She then held out her hand for him to shake. She swallowed and said, "My name is Sonya, but my friends call me Sunny."

Aaron shook her hand.

"So, why do you think I need help finding a house?"

Sonya took another drink of his soda.

"You've got Kansas plates on your car and a newspaper opened up to rental houses in your seat." She pointed at the folded paper beside him.

"Oh," he said, seeming a bit embarrassed.

"What sort of place are you looking for?" she asked, with the last bite of hamburger still in her mouth.

"Well, apartments are out. I play bass guitar, and even though I haven't played for a while, I'd like to get back into it."

Sonya's eyes widened.

"No lie? You play guitar? I can't believe it! That is sooo far-out! Wait till my friends hear that I'm dating a guy named Spyder, and he plays guitar!"

Aaron again sat back a little, "Dating?"

Sonya's smile fell a bit, "Yeah, well just to keep things simple. Don't go getting your hopes up. I mean not that something couldn't happen, but it's just for appearances."

Aaron scratched the side his head. "Appearances?"

"Yeah, sure. It's like this, Spyder. I'm a super-hot fox. You're.... well, a so-so looking guy. The plus side is you've got a rad name and a nice car. And the fact that you play guitar doesn't hurt matters.

"But I don't just hang out with guys to help them find a house. If my friends see me with you, it's got to be dating, at least, understand? I mean, I still have a ... sort of, good reputation to uphold.

"Plus, it will really help you out. I mean, you don't want people to think you're, you know."

Aaron continued to stare at Sonya with an expression of disbelief.

"That I'm what?" he finally asked.

"Well, you know, not interested in women. I mean, if you've got a beautiful woman riding around with you and you tell people you're not dating her, they'll think you must not be interested in women."

Aaron glanced back around, again seeming to hope her friends would show up and take her with them. Again, this didn't happen.

Sonya took another drink of his soda. Then gave him an innocent smile.

Aaron rubbed his chin.

"So, you're going to let me help you?" she asked.

Aaron looked at her for several seconds, seeming reluctant to say what he had to. Finally, he replied, "Actually, I can't refuse your help."

She smiled. "Now, that's more like it. That's the way a girl expects to be treated."

Aaron again expressed dismay but managed a slight smile.

"Here's the plan. You take me home and then pick me up first thing in the morning. We'll find you a great place. I know this area really well."

Just then, one of the carhops skated up to the vehicle next to Aaron's. Turning, she noticed Sonya.

"Hey, Sunny!" She handed the tray to the driver of the car next to Aaron's. She then turned back to Sonya as the driver took the items off the tray.

"Hi, Lindsey! Hey, this is my boyfriend, Spyder!" She pointed to Aaron.

"Hi, Spyder, that's a groovy name." Lindsey leaned over and waved to Aaron, who smiled a little, waved and then rubbed his forehead.

"Hey, if you know of any bands that need a guitar player, let me know. Spyder is looking for a band."

"Bass… guitar!" Aaron said, leaning down a little.

Lindsey was taking the money from the customer next to them, but as soon as they told her to "keep the change," she turned to them again.

"That's really far-out! Yeah, I'll check around and tell you if I hear of something." She then waved bye and skated off.

"You see, Spyder. You'll have a place to live and a lot of friends with me around. And who knows, if you play your cards right, we might be dating for real someday." She smiled and drank the last of his soda.

Aaron expelled a long breath and then started the car.

"Yeah, that would be something." He glanced at her again. "If you're going to ride with me, you may want to buckle up."

She looked at him. "You're kidding, right?"

Aaron smiled, as if he were joking. Then he put the car in reverse and backed out of the parking spot.

The following morning, he picked Sonya up and drove to a cafe. He bought her breakfast and tried to read the newspaper, though it was difficult as Sonya spoke almost nonstop between bites.

Later, they drove around to various houses, looking at each one.

Sonya would often say, "No, that one is not nearly hip enough," or, "We'll keep that one in mind, but it's really not the pad for you."

That evening, they were sitting at another cafe. Aaron sat across from her as she talked about a "flake" boyfriend from her past, describing the entire relationship to be mostly a "drag."

As Aaron watched her, he began to see a glowing around her face and upper body. As he studied this radiance, which he now recalled from his training to be her aura, he completely lost track of what she was saying.

Her aura was a very beautiful pinkish-purple color. This he also recalled meant she had an innocent and trusting nature. He smiled slightly as he examined her.

"So, anyway I told him..." Sonya stopped mid-sentence as she noticed the odd expression on Aaron's face.

"Are you listening to me, Spyder?"

Still, Aaron stared at her with a peculiar smile. She waved her hand in front of his face, and this pulled him from the apparent trance-like state.

"What? Oh, I'm sorry," he said.

"You had me totally tuned out, didn't you?" Her face expressed anger.

"Uhm, yeah, I'm sorry, I guess I did."

She stared at him for several seconds. Then she began to smile.

"That's sooo sweet. You really are a sly one, you know that?"

Now Aaron became a bit confused. "I am?"

"Yes, you are... you were so focused on admiring me that you didn't hear anything I said. I'm going to have to watch out for you." She gave him a sultry smile and then took another bite of her food.

Aaron smiled as well and nodded. Though he had initially been concerned about her helping him, as his training was slowly returning, he knew she was in some way meant to assist him. By perceiving her aura, it was for certain he was on the right path. Her presence was bringing him closer to his primary task, and by doing so, his skills and training would continue to return.

The following day, they went through a similar routine. Through Sonya's abundant conversation skills, Aaron learned she was nineteen-years old. Her mother and father had been separated for several years, and she lived with her mother. She had "barely" graduated high school because the boys would never leave her alone. She loved rock-and-roll music and "really, really" wanted to see the Rolling Stones in concert.

As they were driving and she was talking, Aaron glanced over to her. She really was a beautiful young woman. As if sensing he was admiring her, she stopped and looked at him, then smiled brightly.

A few hours later, they pulled up to a large building on Bayou Street. It appeared to have been used for several things over its lifetime. There were a few faded signs painted over the red brick exterior. A large rolling door could be seen not far from a steel walk-in doorway.

"I think this is it, Spyder," Sonya said as she studied the old building.

Aaron's face twisted slightly, though she didn't see it.

After a short wait, the owner pulled up in a black-and-white Cadillac. A few minutes later, they were walking around a large, open-bay room.

"There's a small living area back over there, through that door. It's got a furnished kitchen area, bedroom and a full bathroom." The man then puffed on his cigar.

"You two thinking of opening a business?" he asked.

Aaron studied the man's aura. It reflected a mostly honest man, though there were some tints of greed as well.

Aaron replied, "I play music. I just need some space, along with a place to live, where I won't bother neighbors."

"Well, you'll have plenty of room here, and no neighbors... Did I mention the deposit?"

Aaron glanced back at the man and could see this was something he had come up with after hearing the building may be used for music.

"Uhm, no, I don't think you mentioned that, but a reasonable deposit will be fine with me."

The man smiled around the cigar protruding from his mouth.

Sonya had wandered over to the living area. She walked through the door and then stepped back out.

"You've got to see this, ss...sweetheart!" she called out.

Aaron smiled at the man, "Excuse me." He then went over to Sonya.

"Sweetheart?"

"Yeah, well, don't get too excited. I just didn't want to call you Spyder while you're doing business. Look at this." She then walked into the living area.

"I do have another name." Aaron said under his breath as he followed behind her. She didn't respond to his remark.

"I think this is it. This is the pad for us... I mean you." She then held out her hand, as if presenting the room.

There was a living area, a bedroom and bathroom attached. The kitchen area was in the corner of the living area.

Sonya was smiling when Aaron's eyes came back around to her.

"You can park your car inside. There's room for a band and lots of guests. We can stay here."

"Wait, us? And we can stay here?" Aaron asked.

"Well, just until I finish helping you find some furniture. By that time, I'll have probably lost interest in you anyway. That's the way it usually works. You are somewhat boring by the way. I'm hoping you can play guitar better than you can have conversations. I mean, if it weren't for you admiring me so much all the time, I'm sure I would have already lost interest."

Sonya then walked to the bathroom and looked in as Aaron rubbed his chin and watched her.

Twenty minutes later, Aaron was handing the man rent and deposit. Then, after signing an agreement, Sonya hugged Aaron and kissed him on the cheek.

The next day, Sonya led them to a second-hand furniture store. Aaron walked over to a queen-sized bed. It was an old iron-post type. As he studied it, Sonya walked over to him.

"I don't like it."

He glanced at her. "Well, maybe I do."

"Well, you're not the one that's going to be sleeping on it. You better go find a couch that looks comfortable."

Aaron stared at her for several seconds.

"All right, you're telling me, I paid the rent and a rather large deposit on a place, where you plan on sleeping in the bed while I sleep on a couch?"

"Yeah, of course! What were you thinking? Wait, noooo, I know what you were thinking. What sort of girl do you think I am? You know, I have half a mind to just call it quits right now. I'm trying to help you, and you're making plans to…," her face twisted in a disgusted manner. "Oh, you really are a naughty boy."

Aaron's mouth dropped, and his eyes widened. He looked around. "So, where are the couches at?"

Sonya smiled and pointed across the large store toward them.

After locating and purchasing a bed Sonya liked and a couch that seemed comfortable enough to sleep on, they then arranged for delivery and went to another store to find additional furniture.

The following evening, Aaron sat on the couch in the large living area. In front of him was the shapely bottom of Sonya. She was leaned over slightly, adjusting the rabbit-ear antenna on top of the TV.

"There, no wait. Uhm... oh, these silly things." She moved her bottom back and forth as she adjusted the antenna.

Aaron smiled a bit as she struggled to get the television station to come in clear.

"Do you think you can get it to work?" She turned to Aaron.

"You know, I'm doing fine right now. You should give it another try. I think you just about have it."

"Really?" she asked. "But you can't see it, can you?"

She moved over a bit, so Aaron could see the screen. There was a fuzzy black-and-white image of an old rerun.

Aaron squinted a little. He then motioned for her to move a little to the left. She did, and this placed her bottom across half the screen.

"There?" she asked.

Aaron squinted again, then motioned for her to move left some more. She did, and this placed her behind directly in front of the screen.

"Perfect," he said.

Sonya's face twisted as she looked at where she was and noticed the fact that her bottom was directly in front of the screen. Her mouth turned down as she realized what he was doing.

"You... scoundrel!" she almost shouted, but then smiled as she came over and attempted to hit him.

Aaron latched onto her wrist before she was able to slap him. He pulled slightly, and she fell onto his lap. They looked into each other's eyes. She then wrapped her arms around his neck and kissed him passionately on the lips.

Aaron didn't sleep on the couch.

The next morning, Aaron sat in the living room wearing a t-shirt and underwear, watching the morning news. The black-and-white picture was fuzzy, but he watched with interest as the announcer relayed grim events happening in Vietnam.

Sonya walked over with a cup of coffee and handed it to him. Her hair was messy. She wore one of Aaron's shirts and nothing else. Soon she had a cup of coffee as well and sat down beside him.

Aaron stood up and turned the TV off. Sitting back down, he asked, "What can you tell me about the Lefevere brothers?"

Sonya grimaced as she held her coffee with both hands close to her chest.

"I already told you, they're flakes. Worse than flakes. They sell drugs and... well, a lot worse I've heard. But people say they have connections with the mafia or mob or something. So, the police don't really bother them."

Aaron took a sip of his coffee and thought about the new information.

"Why do you want to know about them?" Sonya asked. Then she sat up a little. "Wait, you're an undercover cop, right?"

He looked at her and chuckled. "No, I'm not an undercover cop."

The excited expression fell from her face. "Bummer, I was hoping you were an undercover cop on a top-secret case." She then took another drink of her coffee.

After expelling a deep breath, Aaron continued, "So, do they go to a lot of parties? Or do they throw parties often?"

She looked at him and squinted her eyes with suspicion.

"You better tell me why you're so interested in those two. If you're not an undercover cop, then you're something."

Aaron stared at her for a few seconds.

"All right, all right, I'll try to explain, as much as possible. I am on a… type of mission. But it's not from the government; it's, well, even higher. You probably wouldn't believe me if I told you who I'm working for.

"I don't know exactly what those two have to do with the mission, but they have something to do with it. I feel fairly certain that I'll need to go through those two to reach my primary objective."

Sonya examined him carefully. She took another drink of her coffee and watched him over the rim of the cup. Finally, she sat her coffee on the end table and replied with a sultry voice, "That really turns me on. I mean, you just got me soooo hot."

74

"What turns you on?"

"The way you tease me with nonsense. You're so far-out!" She then moved into his arms. "If it's top-secret stuff, I understand… really. You don't have to make up a bunch of bogus stuff; just tell me it's top secret."

She started kissing him all over. Again, they went to the bedroom.

Soon, Sonya's friends began to drop in. And, as time went by, there were more and more of them hanging around what was being called; the warehouse.'

Aaron and Sonya put some couches and chairs they had found at yard sales around the open area. Then, a guitar player by the name of Rick came by. Soon Rick and Aaron were playing some tunes.

A week later they found a drummer, and with the three musicians, more people began to hang around.

As the weeks went by, Aaron's training continued to return, and he found his spiritual skills to be sharpening with every day that passed.

He took the Plymouth to the Lefevere brothers' garage for an oil change one day.

As he examined the two brothers, along with the other mechanics in the garage, he saw they had almost no aura. Their faces expressed a black-skull image of death. They acted civilized and friendly, but Aaron could see the true state of their being. It was dark and evil.

CHAPTER SIX:

Razing the Hellion

Several weeks after Aaron's visit to the Lefevere brothers' garage, a singer came to the warehouse and completed the band.

Two months after moving into the warehouse, Aaron's band finished playing several songs. There were at least a hundred people in the building. It had become a popular hangout for the party crowd. As the song wrapped up and the crowd applauded, the singer spoke over the microphone, "Thank you. We need to take quick break. I've got a bad case of cottonmouth."

As the band sat their instruments down and moved into the crowd, Sonya approached Aaron with another young woman. Sonya had recently begun wearing miniskirts, and Aaron couldn't help but admire her legs. Noticing this, she smiled and winked at him.

"Spyder, this is Randy. She wanted to ask you something." Sonya then turned where the young woman couldn't see and gave Aaron a sour face.

The young woman smiled. She also wore a short skirt, yet her overall appearance was of being provocative. Her hair was dark brown, and her tight-fitting top displayed with clarity that she was not wearing a bra.

"Well, I was telling Sunny that my cousin, Marcus Lefevere, is having a big party at his place next Saturday. I could invite you two, if you want."

Aaron immediately perked up. "You're inviting us to your cousin Marcus's party?" he asked.

"Yeah, sure, if you want to come," Randy replied with a smile.

"We would love to come. Thank you, Randy," Aaron said.

The young woman smiled and then replied, "If anyone asks, just tell them Randy invited you."

Aaron nodded, "Thanks again."

Randy walked away. Sonya turned to Aaron.

"I thought you might be interested in that. You owe me."

"I owe you what?" he asked.

"I don't know, but it's big and expensive, that's for sure."

He smiled and then, leaning over, gave her a kiss.

Sonya smiled a little. "That's not going to cover much, mister." She then walked away.

As he watched her, she wagged her behind a little, then turning, gave him a quirky smile, indicating she was aware he was observing her.

The following Saturday afternoon, Aaron and Sonya dressed for the party. As she put on another short skirt, Sonya whined, "I can't believe you're taking me to one of those flakes' parties! Those people are trash, Spyder!"

She turned to him and then buttoned her skirt. "Did you hear me?"

Aaron looked at her and smiled.

"Ahhgg." She then went to a wardrobe and pulled out a blouse.

An hour later, the two were rolling past the drive of a large two-story house. There were cars all along the driveway and even parked in the yard of the mansion.

After he pulled past the entrance, he moved to the next block.

"Where are you going? That was the house," Sonya said.

"I know, but we're parking a little farther away."

She looked at him with dismay. "Spyder, I'm wearing heels!"

He glanced at her. "I'm sorry, sweetheart, but I've got a feeling we don't want to be parked very close."

Shaking her head, she again whined under her breath, "You really, really owe me for this one."

Once they found a parking place, about a block and a half from the Lefevere house, they began walking.

Aaron held Sonya's arm as she mumbled to herself in frustration and carefully made her way along the sidewalk.

Then up the long drive they went. Cars passed by them, and as they came closer to the house, loud rock-and-roll music was heard.

The two walked up the steps, and at the front door, they met a large man who appeared to be a guard. He held out his hand to stop them.

"Randy invited us," Aaron said.

The man looked them over, then waved them inside.

As they entered, a window was heard shattering somewhere toward the back of the house.

Walking through the large front room, they noticed several people sitting at a table, snorting white powder.

Continuing through the hallway, a young woman wearing shorts and a bra jogged past them, laughing. They looked at each other and then proceeded to a very spacious room toward the middle of the house.

The ceiling was high in this room, and a balcony ran around the second-floor area.

As the two made their way past a multitude of people, one of the Lefevere brothers stepped out to the balcony area. He was the short, sickly looking one. Sonya leaned over and identified him as Marcus Lefevere.

"Hey, everybody, this is a tape of Bitter Black! " He then waved a reel-to-reel tape around and everyone except Aaron and Sonya shouted with joy.

A few minutes after Marcus stepped into the room behind him, the music changed.

As the tape began to play, Aaron put a hand to his ear, almost in pain. He immediately identified the singer as not from the physical plane. The vocals were loud and aggressive. It was something he had not heard before.

"What's wrong?" Sonya asked as Aaron again winced from the song.

"Not my kind of music," Aaron replied.

"Yeah, it stinks! Everything around here stinks. Look at that!" she said, raising her voice loud enough to be heard over the music.

Aaron looked to where she had pointed. In the corner was a small group of people, and looking closer, he could see one was sticking a hypodermic needle in another's arm.

"Can we leave now? I told you this was a bad idea."

"No, not yet."

As he answered her, Marcus came down the stairs.

A few minutes later, Sonya casually pointed to Matson Lefevere who stood in another area with a small group of people. He was the larger, burly brother of Marcus. Aaron also noticed several others from the party where he first saw the two.

Taking Sonya's arm, they began moving around to another area where he could view the Lefevere group better. Passing a large tub full of ice with beer of various brands, he pulled one out. Sonya stopped and, taking more time to choose, finally selected a beer and then walked quickly to catch up to Aaron.

"Who's that?" Aaron asked, pointing out a woman that sat on a large sofa beside Marcus.

"That's Marcus's wife... well, I don't know that they're married."

Across from Marcus sat a young woman of sixteen or seventeen. She held a glass of something, and her eyes were lowered, as if she were ashamed or depressed. Aaron noticed that Marcus continued to eye this young woman.

After taking the top from the beer and drinking a small amount, Aaron asked, "What about the girl there? Who's she?"

Sonya expelled a sigh, seeming to lose patience, but she moved over a little and looked.

"That's Mandie....or Mindy, yeah, Mindy I'm pretty sure; she's the daughter of Marcus's wife or girlfriend… whatever she is to him." She took a drink of her beer and continued, "The rumor is Marcus has a thing for Mindy, and her mother lets him… you know… Isn't that sick?"

After observing a few more seconds, Aaron replied, "From the way he's looking at her, I suspect the rumor is true." He took another drink of his beer and went on, "I feel the time has come for Marcus to see who he really is. Tonight, he'll get an accurate insight of the real Marcus Lefevere."

Sonya nodded her head, "Great, can we go now?"

"No. In fact, I think you'll need to wait by yourself for a little while."

As he said this, Marcus stood up and took Mindy's hand. She appeared frightened and looked over to her mother, who simply smiled and nodded to her, as if she should go with Marcus.

"What? Spyder, I don't want to be here at all, now you're going to leave me… by myself?"

Aaron watched as Marcus led Mindy over to the stairs. Mindy's head was lowered as she was almost pulled up to the second floor by Marcus.

"It can't be helped. Stay around here. I'll be back to get you as soon as I can." He then handed her his beer.

Sonya glared at him as he walked away. He smiled a little, and she turned his beer up, finishing the remainder off in one long drink.

As Marcus stepped to the top of the balcony, almost pulling Mindy behind, Aaron started up the stairs.

Marcus and Mindy turned down a hallway as Aaron passed several people and then turned down the same hallway.

There was not much light in the hall. He could see Marcus and Mindy stepping into a room. Aaron walked down the hall, moved into the shadows and waited.

For around thirty-five minutes Aaron leaned against a wall. Behind the door, he could hear Marcus yelling on several occasions. Then he heard someone being slapped and Mindy crying. Again, it became quiet.

Aaron carefully moved to a position across the hall from the doorway. Finally, after another short wait, the door unlocked. As the door began to open, Aaron reached up and wiped his forefinger across his eye, making sure to get moisture on it.

As Mindy walked out, she looked at Aaron with surprise. He smiled to her but could see she had been crying and one side of her face appeared to be bruised.

The young woman lowered her head in shame and moved on down the hall. Aaron stepped closer to the door.

Marcus stepped out of the door backwards. He was buckling his belt and trying to close the door as well.

As Marcus turned, Aaron placed his finger on the man's forehead. Marcus immediately froze, his eyes appeared to be pulled to the top of his head. His mouth dropped open.

Aaron held his finger on the man's head for several seconds and then said to him, "See."

When Aaron pulled his finger away, Marcus jerked. He began to blink uncontrollably. He shook his head and his eyes widened. He jerked again and began to make an odd moaning sound.

Aaron walked toward the stairs. He glanced back, and Marcus was running his hands through his hair, then he took a handful of hair and pulled it up, as if trying to pull it all out.

Aaron moved back down the stairs. He glanced over to where Mindy was. She was watching him. Then Aaron noticed that Matson was watching Mindy. He then looked up the stairs and straight at Aaron. His face displayed the black skull image that Aaron knew to be representative of a dark soul.

As Aaron moved toward the bottom level, Matson and Mindy both continued to watch him.

He stepped back through the crowd and made his way to where he had left Sonya.

As he came up to her, she was finishing off another beer. When she saw him, she laughed, somewhat to herself, "Well, you did come back." Her speech was slightly slurred, and he realized she had already had several beers too many.

"I'll have you know several men have already offered to take me home."

Aaron nodded and put his arm around her waist. As she giggled and put her arm around him, Aaron turned his attention to the top of the stairs.

"You're a sly one. You knew I wouldn't run off, didn't you?" she asked in a sultry voice.

Aaron didn't answer. He continued to watch the balcony area around the top of the stairs. The music continued to permeate the air.

"Spyder...?"

Just then, Marcus walked out to the balcony. His face was stretched, and his eyes were wide. He looked over the people below and raised a large pistol in the air.

Aaron moved Sonya behind him. She hadn't noticed Marcus and began to kiss the back of Aaron's neck.

"Stay behind me," he said.

Sonya moaned and continued to nuzzle up to the back of Aaron's neck.

Marcus turned and kicked in the door of the room he had entered earlier to play the tape. Several shots rang out, and Aaron felt Sonya jump. The music stopped, as if Marcus had targeted the audio device. Some people ran from the room while others stopped what they were doing and looked to the top of the stairs. Marcus came back out to the rail of the balcony.

"MAKE IT STOP!!" he shouted, then waved the gun, as if he was going to shoot someone below. Several women let out cries of fear.

"DO YOU SEE IT? DO YOU SEE IT? MAKE IT STOP!!" he shouted again. Then he shot out a large light from the ceiling, and glass fell to the floor.

More people began to scream and run from the room. Sonya began to tremble and pulled on Aaron.

"Let's go," she said, with a wavering voice.

"No, stay behind me," Aaron said as Marcus began to half walk and half stumble down the stairs.

"Don't you see it?" he asked again as panic took over the large house.

He fired a shot into the air, and this caused more chaos. Matson, Mindy and those with Marcus also moved cautiously from the room, seeming to be as frightened as the guests.

Then, as the last few people scampered out and Aaron stood alone, with Sonya crouching behind him, Marcus waved the gun around, searching for a target. He moved it past Aaron, as if not seeing him. His eyes blinked again, expressing pain. Turning to a large window, he shot it out, and glass flew all around.

"Can't you see it?" he seemed to say to himself, since there was only him, Aaron and Sonya left in the large room.

Sonya continued to tremble behind Aaron, who remained standing, keeping his eyes on Marcus.

Marcus shook his head again, as if trying to shake something from his hair. He put the gun to his head and held it there for several seconds. Then he pulled it down and shouted, "DON'T YOU SEE IT?"

Marcus then moved on toward the front of the house. Aaron reached around and pulled Sonya to his front. She was crying, and her makeup was running down her face.

"Let's go," he said.

"That's what I said over an hour ago!" she almost yelled through the sobs.

Making their way to the back of the house, they passed by people hiding in corners and behind counters. They found the back door as another shot rang out toward the front of the house. Through the backyard they moved and then on through a neighbor's yard. As they reached the street, sirens could be heard moving to the front of Marcus Lefevere's house.

Under the hazy streetlights, Aaron assisted Sonya toward the Plymouth. She stumbled a little as she was still crying and obviously drank too much. Several more police cars screamed by them with sirens blaring.

Once they were in the car, Sonya completely broke down in tears, holding her face in her hands. Aaron rolled the window down and listened.

The night sky was lit up from the lights of the police cars. A bullhorn was heard, but Aaron couldn't make out what was being said. A few minutes later, five or six shots could be heard. Sonya jumped and squealed.

"What was that?" she asked, as she wiped tears from her eyes.

Aaron reached down and started the car. He put it into gear and began to pull away.

"It seems Marcus wasn't able to accept the truth of who he was."

"What? What are you talking about?"

Aaron smiled a little and then reached over and caressed her cheek. She laughed a bit and then cried again. Once they returned to the warehouse, he got her to bed and stayed with her until she fell asleep.

CHAPTER SEVEN:

A Matter of Werewolves

The following morning, Aaron sat on the couch drinking coffee and watching the fuzzy images on the black-and-white TV. Sonya walked in wearing one of Aaron's shirts.

As she sat down by Aaron, the morning news announced Marcus Lefevere being shot by police the previous night. Then it went on to report a large amount of heroin being found in the Marcus Lefevere residence.

Sonya rubbed her head as she listened and watched the police busily reeling yellow tape around the front doors of the house.

"You see, that's why I didn't want to go to his party. The guy was a major flake. I mean, I hate that he got shot, but did you see him? He was all doped up on heroin or something. I don't know how we didn't get killed!"

She then stood up and went over to make herself a cup of coffee. Aaron watched her and smiled as she again rubbed her messed-up hair and then scratched her naked bottom.

Things returned to the semi-normal state they were in before the Lefevere party. Until Aaron's birthday came around.

Aaron reclined back on the couch and watched Sonya as she danced about on the coffee table in front of him. She smiled and, pulling down on her short dress, her underwear suddenly dropped to her ankles. She stepped out of one side and then, with her foot, tossed the panties onto Aaron, hitting him square in the face.

He smiled and examined the pink underwear as she began to dance around again. Then there was a knock on the front door.

"Oh, it's here!" Sonya said and then, carefully stepping off the coffee table, tried to run in her high heels but slowed and walked quickly to the front door.

Aaron stood up and started to follow her. Realizing he still held her panties in his hand, he stopped and tossed them on the coffee table.

At the front door, Sonya was thanking a man and then shut the door. She was holding something, and as she turned, Aaron could see it was a small, brindle-and-white puppy.

"Oh, you are a little sweetheart. Let's go meet your daddy." Sonya pet the puppy's head as she walked toward Aaron.

"Wait a minute, Sunny. If you're thinking what I think you're thinking, it's absolutely no!"

Aaron waved his hands in the air and turning, walked back toward the living area. Sonya followed him.

"Spyder! It's your birthday present. Well, one of them. You still get... you know." The puppy licked her face. "Just look at her. She's sooo cute. And, she can be a watchdog."

"No, I don't need a dog. What makes you think I need a dog?" Entering the living area, he walked over and opened the refrigerator as Sonya sat down on the couch, still cuddling the puppy.

"It's a full-blood Boxer. Judy's brother raises them, and he said they're great watchdogs. And, when I saw this one, I just knew she was for you. Spyder, he didn't want to give this one up. I almost had to do something naughty for it. But I used the money you gave me last week instead."

Aaron walked over to her with a cold ginger ale in his hand. He expelled a long breath of air, then looked at the puppy and shook his head.

"I don't want a dog. Believe me, you're enough to take care of. I can't keep up with another female around here."

He sat down on the other end of the couch and took a drink of his soda. Sonya began to pout, and the puppy crawled from her arms.

As Aaron was lowering the soda bottle, the puppy waddled up to him and began to crawl into his lap. Aaron started to push it aside but stopped. He sat his drink on the coffee table.

He picked the puppy up and looked at its eyes. The left one was baby blue, and the other was a beautiful cream color.

Almost under his breath, Aaron said, "Exousia."

Sonya looked at him, "What?"

Aaron continued to examine the puppy but replied, "Authority angels or warrior angels. They're known as Exousia in old Greek."

Sonya expressed confusion, but she scooted over to Aaron.

"So, you like it?"

Aaron looked at her and smiled, "Yeah, I like it. It's just like you said; she was meant for me."

Sonya immediately smiled brightly.

"I told you! But we're not going to name her that silly Greek stuff you talked about."

She took the puppy and, looking it over, said, "How about Suzie, for short?"

The puppy licked her face, and Sonya giggled.

Aaron smiled, "I guess she likes it."

She laughed and, turning, kissed him.

***

Four months after his birthday, Aaron and Sonya sat on a beach together. Aaron tossed a stick into the water, and Suzie waded out into the waves, took hold of the stick and brought it back.

Sonya looked at Aaron from behind her round sunglasses. She chuckled a little as Suzie played tug-of-war with the stick, finally relinquishing it for Aaron to throw again.

As Suzie waded into the waves again, Sonya watched and spoke softly, "You know, my mom says you're dangerous to be around. She said I should find another boyfriend."

Aaron looked at Sonya for several seconds, then replied, "You should always listen to your parents."

She turned in surprise. "You think I should find another boyfriend?"

Suzie brought the stick back. Aaron took it and tossed it to the edge of the waves.

"The day will come when it will be too dangerous for you to be around me."

He looked at her, and though he couldn't see her eyes behind the glasses, he knew she was close to crying. Her mouth twisted a little, and she looked down at the sand between her legs.

For a moment, only the sound of the waves was heard. Then Sonya said softly,

"I don't want that day to come."

Suzie brought Aaron the wet stick. He threw it again. Then he turned to Sonya, "Nevertheless, it will come."

She wiped a tear and turned away from him. Nothing else was said.

***

Weeks passed and Sonya began to proclaim Suzie was able to understand everything Aaron said to her. He did, in fact, talk to Suzie as if she were human. Everyone that hung out at the warehouse expressed amazement at the dog's intelligence.

As spring arrived, Aaron received an interesting invitation.

"Don't tell me you're really thinking about going." Sonya stared at Aaron as he looked the paper over.

"Yeah, actually I've been waiting for this," he replied.

"Spyder... really? Do you recall what happened the last time we went to one of those nutty Lefevere parties?"

She almost stomped over to the kitchen counter. Suzie followed her and sat down beside her legs. Sonya took a dog treat from a box on the counter and handed it to Suzie.

"Besides, Matson is twice Mindy's age. The skuzz. What is that all about anyway? He's marrying Mindy now that Marcus is dead, and he's inviting you to his engagement party? You don't even know him, do you?"

Aaron folded the invitation back up.

"Their entire criminal operation folded after Marcus died. He's been rebuilding all this time. He knows something about me, and this is the bait. That poor girl is simply a tool for Matson. She's been used and abused by both brothers. I sense he knows this will get my attention."

Sonya again stared at him in disbelief for several long seconds, then almost shouted,

"You're trippin'! You know that? Totally trippin'! I know you've got some sort of crazy, secret thing going on. I don't care if it's real or not, but I do care about you, all right?"

She then stormed out of the room. Suzie followed until she came to Aaron. She then stopped and, sitting down, stared at him.

"What?" he asked her.

Suzie whined. Aaron shrugged his shoulders and looked at her with a puzzled expression.

"Hey, you know what I'm up against. What am I supposed to do?"

Suzie whined again and then let out a quick bark. Aaron shook his head.

"Yeah, all right, I know what you want. You want me to be soft and gentle with her, right?"

Again, Suzie whined, seeming to confirm his assessment. Letting out a long breath of frustration, Aaron shook his head and again looked at Suzie.

"Yeah, fine, I'll try to be more teddy bearish. All right?" He then walked to the refrigerator.

Suzie went to find Sonya and soon lay with her head in her lap.

Two weeks later, Aaron and Sonya were dressed for the engagement party. As he opened the passenger door for her, he noticed she wore a short white skirt with high-top black boots, a tight-fitting black top with frills and a small white vest.

Before closing the car door, he couldn't help but admire her. For several seconds he looked her over. Noticing he wasn't shutting the door, she turned to him, "You just can't keep your eyes off me, can you?"

Aaron smiled, and Sonya smiled.

"And you know I love it!" she added.

He nodded and winked at her, then shut the door and moved over to the driver's side.

Twenty minutes later, they were driving down a long stretch of dirt road. As they arrived at Matson's house, both cringed a bit.

The Matson Lefevere home was a very old house and appeared to have been around since the Civil War. It was a two-story, plantation-styled structure.

"You've got to be joking? This place is spooooky," Sonya said as the car stopped.

After a short stroll, the two walked up the steps, and Aaron handed a servant their invitation. Once the invitation was confirmed, he directed them to the backyard. They nodded and went inside the dimly lit structure.

Immediately, Aaron spotted several ghosts wandering around.

"I wonder if this place is haunted," Sonya said, not having the ability to see the things Aaron saw, but perhaps sensing the ghosts.

"Yeah, it's haunted for certain, by three ghosts at least," Aaron replied and then subtly waved to one, which was dressed in attire from the turn of the century and appeared to observe the two guests curiously.

Sonya glanced at Aaron with an odd expression. Then she moved closer to him as they made their way to the back yard.

A large group of people were assembled in the rear area of the old mansion. Farther back was a pond with a few ducks swimming in it.

As the two moved down the back steps, Sonya held Aaron's arm, and he felt her shudder.

"I thought the crowd at Marcus's party was bad. This bunch looks like the Adams family multiplied by twenty."

She was not far off. As Aaron examined the faces of these people, he saw only black, sunken skull images, which indicated these were dark souls filled with evil.

The only person that still had a neutral aura was Mindy. As they approached, she meekly examined the other guests but appeared not to notice Aaron or Sonya.

Aaron noticed Mindy's aura was still an orange-and-blue color, indicating a troubled soul, but not evil.

As they moved about and attempted to socialize, Sonya took a glass of wine, and Aaron took a beer offered by servants.

Studying the layout of the gathering, Aaron spotted six large and aggressive dogs dispersed around the party grounds. They were each being held with leashes by men.

Sonya took a drink of her wine and then nudged Aaron's arm. Turning, he saw a well-dressed Matson Lefevere walking out of the old house and toward the gathering.

Several rough-looking men accompanied him, and Mindy was quickly ushered over to Matson. He then moved around, greeting the guests, and was soon walking toward Aaron and Sonya.

As soon as Matson noticed Aaron, he smiled very arrogantly. As Mindy passed by, she also took notice of Aaron. Her face expressed the same wonder it had the night of the party at Marcus's house.

Soon, music was blaring, and fires were set around the large backyard. The men holding the dogs on leashes wandered about, as if on guard. They would move past Matson, and he would pet the dogs.

As the sun began to set, Aaron watched Matson closely. As he observed the man, he began to see something very alarming. The black skull image he normally had was slowly changing.

As this was occurring, he also noticed Mindy's aura changing to one of extreme fear. Matson would continually pull her to him, yet she obviously sensed something very frightening.

"So, we've made an appearance. Can we go now?" Sonya asked as the night became complete.

Aaron almost didn't hear what she said. As he studied Matson, he could see the spirit features of his face changing to something that was not human.

Then, unexpectedly, Sonya put everything into perspective for Aaron.

"Hey, look at that, it's a full moon. You know what they say full moons are good for?"

Aaron looked up into the night sky to see a full moon rising. He looked back at Matson and now realized the features of a wolf were developing. Though no one else could see this spiritual transformation, it was obvious Mindy had been around it before and was very frightened.

Glancing back to Sonya, Aaron finally answered her, "Werewolves?"

She was taking a drink of her wine and almost choked. After struggling to swallow, she held her hand to her chest and looked at him with a puzzled expression. "Werewolves? I was going to say they're good for love! But what do you know about werewolves?"

Aaron continued to watch Matson as he spoke.

"They're the product of a witch and an evil spirit. The wolf trait is also known as Lycanthrope. The evil spirit couldn't inhabit a human being, so it entered a wolf. The witch and the wolf then copulated under a full moon to strengthen the conception."

As he said this, Matson tossed his beer bottle and motioned for Mindy to get him another. The transformation was almost complete, and Aaron could now clearly see the shadowy wolf image. Mindy went to get another beer as Matson's rage increased. Aaron could sense the anger developing in the man. Matson looked at Aaron again, and his eyes belayed the reason he had wanted Aaron to come. He would use his werewolf strength and fury to destroy Aaron.

Aaron continued as Sonya stared at him with a blank and lost expression.

"Since the first werewolf abomination was produced on that night many millennia ago, the trait shows up from time to time in persons with extremely evil souls. The only known way to defeat one is an ancient Latin recital, which can force the evil spirit from the human body. The problem is having the time and ability to recite it to a violent beast."

As he finished saying this, Mindy brought a beer to Matson. Sonya shook her head in dismay, as Aaron continued to watch the events across the lawn.

"That's not right at all! It takes a silver bullet to kill a werewolf! You don't know much about werewolves, do you?"

As she said this, Matson took a drink of his beer. His face grimaced, and Aaron knew what was about to happen. He handed his beer to Sonya.

"Unfortunately, I didn't know I would have to fight one tonight."

As Sonya's face twisted again, she asked, "What?"

Matson threw the beer to the ground.

"THIS BEER IS HOT!" he yelled at Mindy. The young girl's face expressed terror.

Aaron began to walk quickly toward the two. Before he reached them, Matson turned and backhanded Mindy, causing her to fall hard to the ground.

Picking up speed, Aaron put his arms out and slammed into Matson, who stumbled and fell onto the ground.

Before he could do anything else, several of Matson's male guests and associates took hold of him. Aaron struggled as they held his arms.

Matson stood up, brushed his clothes off and gave Aaron an evil smile.

"Well, well. It's the Spyder man. I was surprised to see you here. I didn't think you was that stupid."

Matson came closer.

"I know you had something to do with Marcus's death. I don't know what, but you're going to pay tonight." He then motioned to the men holding Aaron, "Let him go. No one interfere; this one's mine."

The men let him go, and Aaron adjusted his shirt. The two began to square off, and a crowd gathered in a circle around them.

Matson suddenly leapt into the air with the energy and agility of a wolf. Landing on Aaron, they tumbled violently to the ground. Then both rolled around to gain an advantage.

The werewolf growled in rage and was soon on top.

Aaron found himself deflecting blow after blow as Matson hovered over him and attempted to pound Aaron's head into the ground with his fists.

Summoning strength from deep within, Aaron pushed Matson off. He then stood quickly as the werewolf immediately attacked again.

This time, Aaron had the chance to set his feet. Rather than being knocked over, Aaron grabbed Matson, and both tumbled to the ground. Again, the two struggled for an edge over each other.

Maneuvering Matson's arm behind him, Aaron was able to hold the werewolf down in a locked position that kept him from moving. As Matson struggled, Aaron put more pressure on his arm, causing Matson extreme pain if he moved.

Then Aaron leaned over and began speaking into Matson's ear. The words he spoke were Latin, and Matson began to writhe about, as if in pain.

With a jerk, the werewolf twisted violently and moved Aaron enough for him to get away. Aaron tried to stand but was immediately tackled by Matson.

The dense Louisiana heat caused both men to perspire and struggle with the thick air. All around him, Aaron could hear dogs barking, along with Matson's friends and relatives shouting for Matson to "kill him!"

Again, Matson hovered over Aaron, hitting him with a violent ferocity. Matson's face now had the fiery image of a wolf in place of an aura. Aaron again reached deep within for strength.

Rolling to his left, Aaron got Matson dislocated from on top of him. As the werewolf was scrambling to retake the advantage, Aaron evaded the attack and leapt on Matson's back.

They fell to the ground, and Aaron got his arm around Matson's neck. Squeezing tightly, he again began to recite the Latin words in Matson's ear. Once again, the werewolf writhed about and growled as if being burned. Aaron held tightly and continued the recitation.

Matson's mouth began to open, and Aaron could see the odd Lycanthrope entity struggling from his mouth. It was black and vile in appearance, though Aaron was the only one who could see it.

The evil spirit struggled to stay in Matson yet could obviously not endure the words Aaron spoke.

"You're killing him! Get off!" One of Matson's guests lunged toward the two. This caused Aaron to stop the recitation. The vile spirit immediately reentered Matson, and he pushed back, causing Aaron to almost lose his hold.

Then several other men came toward the two, prepared to assist Matson. Endeavoring to hold onto the werewolf, Aaron shouted with the force of his spirit behind the words, "GET BACK!"

The power knocked the men off their feet and several yards back.

Again, Aaron began reciting the ancient Latin words. Again, Matson fought, as if being tortured.

As Matson's guests picked themselves up and expressed shock, the vile spirit again began to squeeze from Matson's mouth. Aaron renewed his recital efforts as the male guests began talking amongst themselves, seeming to discuss another attack.

Matson squirmed and growled as the black and disgusting Lycanthrope spirit slowly exited him. As the men were about to attack Aaron again, the vile abomination could endure no more and flew from Matson's mouth. It could not survive in the physical realm either and flying to one of the large dogs, crawled into its mouth.

The dog shook and growled as the evil spirit entered it. Once fully inside, the dog took off running at full speed. The man that was holding the leash was dragged across the lawn for several yards before getting his hand loose.

As Aaron let go of Matson and struggled to his feet, trying desperately to catch his breath, the dog ran at full speed into the pond. While the shocked guests watched, the dog swam to the middle and drowned, seemingly on purpose.

Only now, as Aaron staggered and his lungs heaved to pull in the thick air, did he notice someone had stopped the loud music.

Half the guests stared at Aaron and Matson while the other half had moved their attention to the pond when the dog ran into it.

Sonya came to Aaron's side, still holding her glass of wine and Aaron's beer. With his mouth dry, Aaron took the beer but kept his eyes on Matson.

Downing the rest of his beer, he then tossed the bottle and began walking toward the house. With his clothes torn and stained from the grass, almost stumbling from exhaustion, he motioned for Sonya to follow as Matson caught his breath and slowly began to stand up.

Without the Lycanthrope trait, Matson was at a loss for what had happened. He obviously knew something was no longer in him and looked around in a confused state.

Aaron still struggled to recover from the confrontation but was now able to straighten up a bit as he walked. He glanced back at all the guests standing around as Matson's face grew twisted with anger.

As no one seemed to know what to do, or what would happen next, Matson yelled out in anger, "Aaaagggghhhhhhh." Yet, his voice was puny and weak compared to what it had been before. He charged toward Aaron.

Knowing the vile spirit had been expelled from Matson, Aaron stopped, turned and stepped back. As Matson came to Aaron swinging, he deflected Matson's blow with his left arm, then swung with his right. The hit Aaron delivered to Matson's face knocked the man completely out. He fell back to the ground unconscious.

Seeming shocked, several of his friends came and began to pull him toward a lawn chair. Aaron shook his right hand to alleviate the pain from striking Matson's face. He turned and stepped close to Sonya, who stood holding her wine glass, expressing shock as well.

"Come on, we'd better get out of here."

She looked at him with both confusion and admiration, then turned and struggled to walk quickly on the lawn due to her high heels.

Aaron held her arm, and they reached the back of the house. As they walked up the steps of the large porch, Mindy walked out from the house and came up to them.

"Thank you," she said gratefully.

Aaron glanced back and could see it was only a matter of time before Matson's friends and associates came after him. He quickly pulled the wallet from his back pocket. Fishing three one-hundred dollar bills out, he handed them to Mindy.

"Here, take this. Get away from here as soon as you can. Don't tell anyone when or where you're going. Not even your mother. Believe me, you'll be much better off starting over than staying around here."

Mindy smiled and seemed to want to say something, but Aaron quickly ushered Sonya through the house and toward the front door, then on to the Plymouth.

As soon as they were in the car, he pulled away from the old mansion and drove back down the country road.

When they were a safe distance from Matson's house, Sonya, still holding the wine glass, said, "Well, that actually went a lot better than I expected."

CHAPTER EIGHT:

The Cavalry Arrives

After a few days of healing up and being nursed by Sonya, Aaron began to rehearse again with the band. As usual, a crowd would gather at the warehouse to listen and party. As Aaron's band got better, he began to locate places to play. The group was eventually named Bayou Juju and became popular in the New Orleans area.

Several weeks after the confrontation with Matson Lefevere, Bayou Juju was playing at a medium-sized tavern in downtown New Orleans to a crowd of around a hundred people, give or take a few.

It was a smoky atmosphere as Aaron picked the bass and often glanced down at Sonya. She sat at the band's table with the girlfriends and friends of the band. Suzie stayed by her and received much attention from others at the table.

Around one-thirty in the morning, Aaron noticed a man enter the tavern. He found a table not far from the band's table and sat down.

The man was dressed in a very nice suit and tie. He seemed out of place in this type of establishment, and Aaron examined him carefully from the stage. What was even stranger than the man's appearance was that he had no perceptible aura. Aaron was a little astounded by this as he had become very adept at perceiving a person's aura, be it good, neutral or evil.

After ordering a drink, the man watched the last few songs before the band wrapped up their show for the night.

Later, as Aaron packed his bass and equipment, Sonya stood close by, holding Suzie's leash. "So, April said her, and Rick are going to his parent's cabin this Tuesday. She's just sooo proud of his parent's cabin. Like that's really a reason to act stuck-up. I tried not to laugh." Sonya stopped talking as Rick, the guitar player, approached with the man in the suit.

"Spyder, this is…, " Rick stopped and looked at the man.

"Oh, I'm so sorry, where are my manners?" the man said.

Reaching into his suit pocket, he produced two business cards. Then he handed one to Rick and one to Aaron.

"Uhm, Mr. Rengo Winters asked to speak with you," Rick said after examining the card. He then walked away.

Aaron also examined the card, which read, "Rengo Winters, inventor, entrepreneur." There was a phone number below that but no address.

"Can I help you, Mr. Winters?"

Rengo smiled slightly, then turned to Sonya. She smiled at him.

"Yes, well, I was hoping to talk with you… alone," he replied.

Aaron glanced at Sonya, who was petting Suzie on the head.

"This is my girlfriend, Sonya," Aaron said.

Again, Rengo smiled and then shook her hand gently.

After taking in a deep breath and seeming uncomfortable, Rengo finally spoke in a soft voice.

"I was hoping you would take a ride with me, where we can speak in private. I wish to discuss your confrontation with the Lycanthrope."

Aaron's face immediately became tensed with apprehension.

"With what?" Sonya asked.

"Nothing, Sunny, could you... uhm, take Suzie home in the Plymouth. I need to speak with Mr. Winters."

Sonya almost shouted as Aaron reached into his pocket to retrieve the keys.

"You're going to let me drive the Plymouth? Far-out!!"

The two men examined the exuberant Sonya for several seconds.

"Just don't wreck it," Aaron said, expressing reservation.

"Very good. I'll take you to your house after our talk," Rengo said.

Aaron handed his bass case to Sonya, and after a quick kiss, he went outside with Rengo.

The two walked a half-block from the tavern, and as they approached a large, black limousine, the driver stepped out and opened the back door.

"Please," Rengo motioned to Aaron, and he climbed into the car.

Once Rengo had entered and the door was shut, the driver pulled the luxurious car onto the road.

Though the streets of New Orleans were rough, the ride was smooth in the limousine. As they moved under the streetlights, Aaron noticed the windows had been smoked for privacy.

Glancing at Rengo, he saw the man was studying his guest with interest. The limo stopped at a red light. As they waited for the light to change, the sound of blaring rock and roll was heard. Then Sonya pulled up on the right side of the limo. She waved at the darkened windows, obviously unaware that Aaron was in the car.

In the back seat, they could see several other young women and Suzie. They were laughing and singing to the loud music. Aaron leaned toward the window for a better look.

"Isn't that your girlfriend?" Rengo asked as Sonya bounced around in the driver's seat.

"Yeah, that's my girlfriend, my dog and my car."

As Aaron said this, the light changed and Sonya stomped on the gas, causing the Plymouth's tires to squeal. It was soon out of sight.

Ten minutes later, the large car was moving beside extravagant mansions along a well-maintained street. Aaron had never been to this side of New Orleans.

Soon the driver turned into an elaborate marble gateway and long drive. Then on to the front of a grand mansion.

Once the car was stopped, the driver opened the door and the two men got out. As they walked up the steps of the porch, the door opened.

A well-dressed maid greeted them as they entered, "Good morning, Mr. Winters."

The woman appeared sleepy but expressed no frustration at having to open the door this early in the morning.

"Thank you, Doris. That will be all. You can rest." After Rengo said this, they continued through the massive front room.

"Yes, sir. Thank you, sir," she replied from behind them.

The two moved into a large game room containing an ornate bar that was well stocked, a pool table and various pinball and arcade machines along the wall.

In the center of the game room sat several plush couches, along with a glass coffee table with crystal containers on it.

"Please have a seat and make yourself at home. I believe you're called… Spyder?" Rengo motioned to the couches and then walked over to the bar.

"Yes, thank you," Aaron replied and sat down.

"Would you like a drink? Or some coffee?"

"Coffee," Aaron said and examined the crystal containers.

Opening the lids one at a time, he found pistachios in one, pecans in another and assorted nuts in the final container. All were still in their shells, but there were several nutcrackers sitting beside the containers.

Soon the smell of fresh-brewed coffee drifted around the room. Aaron took the lid off the pistachios and began opening the nuts by hand. As he was eating them one at a time, Rengo came over and sat a cup of coffee down. He then went back to the bar. Soon he returned with a cup of coffee for himself and a small tray with sugar and creamer.

As Aaron put cream and sugar in his drink, Rengo sat down across from him, took a sip of his coffee and began, "You know, there's almost no information available regarding your kind. The mystic warrior is so shrouded in mystery that, when asked, theologians and scholars suggest you don't exist and never have."

Aaron studied Rengo for several long seconds. He then sat the spoon on the table, lifted his cup and took a drink. Rengo continued, "To be sitting and talking with one of Michael's own is... well, something extraordinary." Rengo paused, as if searching for an indication of Aaron's thoughts. He then continued, "I've often thought of your kind as 'God's Ninjas.' This was, of course, before having met one. Truthfully, you're not exactly what I expected."

Rengo took another sip of his coffee and then stared at his guest.

After studying Rengo with obvious curiosity, Aaron again began to open the pistachio nuts and eat them. Only the sound of Aaron opening the nuts could be heard for several long seconds.

Both men took turns examining each other. As Aaron offered no comment, Rengo finally continued, "There is a bit of information I uncovered, through much effort. It seems there were twelve of your kind at Qumran, when the Romans attacked that community of Essenes. With only twelve mystic warriors, the Essenes held off a Roman legion for months. It was such an embarrassment, the Romans struck it from all writings and executed all who knew of it. Well, almost all, obviously."

Still Aaron said nothing. He continued to eat pistachios and study Rengo.

After taking another drink of his coffee, Rengo expelled a breath of air, seeming to lose patience. He sat back in the couch and stared at Aaron.

Once again, only the sounds of Aaron opening the nuts disturbed the silence. Then Rengo sat back up. He clasped his hands together and continued the one-sided conversation, "Well, regardless of anything else, I do know that you crossed the valley of death. From my understanding, it's a must for your kind."

Aaron stopped opening his nut. His face became stern, and he again studied Rengo very closely.

Smiling at the sudden change, Rengo continued, "Yes, the valley of death. I don't imagine that's something one would forget."

Aaron slowly returned to opening and eating pistachios. But he watched Rengo very closely now.

"I happened to have learned this from a very reliable source, so, I don't doubt the information. And I must say, I feel very humbled to be sitting with someone that has strolled across the valley of death."

Rengo then smiled again and picked his coffee back up. As he took a drink, he watched Aaron with interest.

For several seconds, there was silence. Aaron examined Rengo curiously as he sat his coffee cup back on the table and, clasping his hands together again, waited for a reply.

Aaron finally sat the two nuts in his hand on the coffee table. He brushed his hands off and straightened up. Then he said, "No one strolls across the valley of death. I was carried across by an Authority Angel, while others defended my pathetic soul from the death wraiths. All I did was cry like a helpless baby."

Rengo smiled a little. He nodded and appeared to be considering Aaron's words. Finally, he replied, "I don't know what I expected as a response, but I think that may be the only answer I would consider to be truthful."

He then leaned over toward Aaron. "My card notes that I'm an inventor and entrepreneur. What it doesn't note is that I'm also an alchemist." He paused and then said, "We're on the same side."

After a few seconds of thought, Aaron nodded slightly and said, "An alchemist, that must be why you have no perceptible aura."

Rengo smiled, "It's good to know the camouflage is working. I believe you have a natural camouflage that comes with your class as a warrior. However, the rest of us must conceal our positive aura with elixirs. You're not the only one that can perceive auras. There are many vile people that can sense a positive aura and often react violently against one. But I'm certainly glad to hear my camouflage elixir is still working."

Aaron smiled a bit, then looked around the large luxurious dwelling.

"It's been said some alchemists have a formula for gold. Seems you might be one of them."

Rengo chuckled, "Well, I don't have that formula, but most alchemists know gold when they see it, regardless of its form."

The clock on the wall chimed four times. Both were obviously tired.

"Would you like to get some rest? I have plenty of spare rooms available as well as anything else you might require, such as shaving equipment or a new toothbrush. I can have the maid bring it to you."

Aaron nodded, "Yeah, that sounds good."

As the two stood up and started walking, Rengo seemed to think of something, "Oh, what about your girlfriend?"

"She'll be all right. She's got an angel watching over her."

Rengo stopped and looked back, "Don't we all?"

Aaron smiled but didn't respond.

Rengo took him to the morning maid and instructed her to show him to a room and bring anything he needed.

That afternoon, Aaron wandered downstairs in a set of clothes the maid had brought him. He was then ushered to a large sitting room where a TV was turned on. As he sat down, a pot of coffee was brought to him by a maid, along with cups, cream and sugar.

He drank his coffee and watched news from Vietnam. It was not going well over there. Briefly, he wondered about Ping. Then Rengo walked into the room. He glanced at the TV as he sat down across from Aaron.

"A terrible thing, war. And it has unfortunately plagued us in some form since the dawn of time." After saying this, Rengo reached over to a console beside his chair and, flipping a switch, turned the television off.

"Yes, it's terrible. And it comes in more forms than most know," Aaron replied.

Rengo continued to examine Aaron as a maid entered with a rolling tray. On the tray was an assortment of fried eggs, sausages and meats. Also, there was a variety of breads and juices.

The two prepared a plate of food and moved over to a small table to eat. As they ate, Rengo once again began the conversation, "I was very impressed to hear about the way you dealt with Matson Lefevere. You may be interested to know; his fiancé has left him. She left a note and disappeared. And after losing the Lycanthrope trait, he has become something of a pushover and 'weak' in his drug and other illegal dealings. In fact, it seems only a matter of time before one of his 'associates' moves to take over the business."

Aaron listened as he ate. After some thought, he asked, "So he really didn't understand the evil sprit that used him as a host?"

"It seems apparent he had a basic knowledge of when the trait gave him power and increased his senses. Other than that, I don't believe he understood the spiritual aspect of what was using him as a host. He seems to think he's lost his nerve after being 'whipped' by you. I suspect he'll continue to seek revenge on you, not only for what happened to him, but for you taking down his brother, Marcus."

Aaron stopped eating. He studied Rengo for several long seconds as he held his fork over the plate. "What makes you think I had anything to do with that?"

"As I told you, I... had a very reliable source. She was like you but not of the same class. She was a messenger. And like prophets and messengers before her, she was forced into a battle she was not equipped to fight."

Rengo expressed great sadness as he peered at his food, then continued, "We feel sad when we hear the story of Joan of Arc. Perhaps the most renowned messenger. She too was pushed into a fight that she did not want to take part in. She did what was asked of her, even though it cost her life. It was not until I lost my own Joan of Arc that I really understood the brutality of this unseen war. One that is being waged all around us and yet unknown by so many."

The room fell silent.

Then Aaron said, "Please tell me about her."

Rengo's lips tightened, and he appeared to be on the verge of tears. He took a deep breath and buffered up. After taking a sip of coffee, he replied, "Victoria was her name, but I always called her Tori. She told me you would come and take down the Lefevere brothers. I didn't realize at the time why she was telling me, but afterwards, I understood that she had already foreseen her own death."

Rengo turned away, struggling to manage the emotions within him. He went on, "She told me not to fall in love, but neither one of us could resist. I can't imagine how difficult it must have been to march off to one's own death. She was braver than any person I've known. She did her duty, even though it wasn't her task."

Aaron asked, "What do you mean, not her task?"

"She told me before she left. Well, it was the last time I was able to talk with her. She said there are some that fail in their tasks. This was why she had to go. I thought she would return. It never occurred to me how deadly her job was. I knew she was a messenger, just as Joan of Arc and many others before her. But that was ancient history. I just, didn't realize how real it was.

"Before she left, she told me a mystic warrior was on the way. She told me that this warrior would take the evil Lefevere brothers down and that this warrior would need my help.

"Later, I found this necklace with a note." Rengo reached into his shirt. He pulled out a gold necklace with a tiny crucifix. "She asked me to hold onto it as she was afraid it might get lost.

"I still didn't get it. I still didn't understand. Not until I got the call.

"She had been found dumped in an alley. She was in a coma, for unknown reasons. Three days later, she was dead. The case was closed as mysterious but no indications of foul play.

"You and I both know she was destroyed through spiritual methods. Her physical body could not withstand the evil she confronted."

"Do you know anything more about her last message?" Aaron asked.

"I've learned much about it since her death. She said little about it before she left. Perhaps because she knew I would do everything I could to stop her if I'd known she would not survive it.

"She did tell me that she was to deliver a final warning to one of the fallen. He crossed into the physical realm and took possession of a human, most likely upon the human's request. You may know that fallen angels are not to possess humans. It is strictly forbidden. Though they can venture into the physical realm in spirit form, they are not to inhabit those God has deemed 'mankind.'

"It seems she knew this message would not go well, but she had already warned this fallen angel before. So, I thought it was nothing extraordinary. After her death, I investigated the situation much more extensively.

"The fallen angel has taken possession of a singer. He is in a band named Bitter Black."

When Rengo stated this, Aaron sat up straight and stared at Rengo, who noticed this.

"You know something of this person?"

"I heard some of the band's music at Marcus's house the night he met his end."

Rengo considered this and continued, "The fallen one has created quite a following of humans. He inhabited a singer by the name of Lewis Hinton around two years ago. Lewis was a struggling artist with a mediocre voice. Suddenly, from seemingly nowhere, he possessed a strong, aggressive singing voice. He became increasingly confident and forceful. This is the time I feel he allowed the fallen one to take possession of his body and mind."

Aaron pushed his plate back a little. Both men remained quiet as the maid came around and refilled their coffee cups. Then she took their plates away.

As Aaron put some sugar in his coffee he replied, "Tori understood her duty. It's unfortunate she was required to deliver an additional message. I don't understand the need for a second message, but there must be a reason for it."

Rengo stirred his coffee.

"Lewis Hinton has protection. I'm not sure what it is, but his band, Bitter Black, is connected to none other than the Lefevere brothers' boss. Which brings us to you."

After taking a drink of his coffee and setting the cup down, Rengo continued, "Have you heard of Sunrise Manor?"

Aaron indicated that he had not.

"It's a large residence... actually, it was, among other things, a plantation. It sets on the edge of New Orleans and has been the residence of August Rollins for much longer than most are aware of.

"The house is infamous for drugs, gambling, alcohol, prostitution, orgies, any sort of decadence imaginable. What's not commonly known, however, is that August Rollins has an acute case of Vampirism. It took a lot of money and investigation to bring this to light."

Aaron leaned over toward Rengo, "A vampire. Tell me everything you know."

"Yes, well, I'm afraid this is no ordinary vampire. He is what would be called a 'vampire lord' in the physical sense, though I suspect there are other names for such a case.

"And, as you may also be aware, vampires, unlike fallen angels, were once human. So, they fall under the protection which all of mankind resides under."

Rengo stood up, picked up his coffee, took a few steps away from the table, and continued, "Contrary to popular belief, they do not suck a person's blood. Rather, they suck and feed off the very essence of one's soul. And though they are not partial to sunlight, it does not destroy them. Also, one doesn't kill a vampire with a stake to the heart. If only it were so easy as that. Again, vampires were once human, and our side is, thankfully, not in the business of assassinations.

"Initially, I thought it impossible to destroy one without breaking a law set forth by the creator. But, over time, and again with much money spent, I've acquired ancient texts containing perhaps the only method for defeating a vampire. Or at least of having hope to put one out of commission."

Rengo glanced at Aaron.

"Shall I proceed?"

"Please do," Aaron replied.

The Greek term is 'Συνέπειες της υπέρβασης του τερματικού σταθμού,' or, in rough translation, 'the consequences of exceeding the boundary.' I'm guessing the boundary was set by God. Though vampires of today may or may not be aware of this 'Achilles heel,' it's doubtful they would ever make the mistakes necessary to fulfill the regulation breech. So, my guess is they are not very concerned about it.

"And, even if they did break all the rules, I'm not certain what would come of it. The ancient texts merely state that once these things occur, the vampire will reap the consequences of God's wrath. Whatever that should be."

Rengo took another drink of his coffee as Aaron listened closely. Then Rengo continued as the evening sun lit up the large room, "First, the vampire must receive a legitimate opportunity to 'change their ways,' so to speak. Of course, they are fully aware of what most call karma, so it's doubtful any vampire in their right mind would accept this offer. Nevertheless, it is a must.

"Then, the vampire must invade a house of God or structure which has been dedicated to God; the translation was a bit vague on that one. But again, this is highly unlikely. Though unafraid of such places, vampires would likely avoid them unless there was a good reason to enter one. So, having one willingly enter such an establishment is doubtful.

"Finally, the vampire must threaten a child of light with harm… whatever that means. Again, the odds of such a thing occurring must be astronomical.

"Vampires understand they are powerful entities. Although they are vain, they're not ignorant. They are known to be vindictive and extremely vengeful. It seems they're completely unable to forgive. If they have a weakness, that would be it.

"Which brings us to you and your recent arrival at this 'hornet's nest.' The Lefevere brothers worked indirectly for August Rollins. I suppose Matson still does, but without the aggressive Lycanthrope trait, he'll soon be overthrown by one of his subordinates.

"Though August will be little affected by the demise of these two vile men, he will hear about it. You've not knocked the hornet nest from the tree, but I suspect you've stirred it up some. You should be very careful from here on."

Aaron leaned back in his chair. He stared out the large windows for several minutes. The maid entered and poured the two more coffee, then left. Finally, Aaron asked, "How difficult would it be to get into Sunrise Manor?"

Rengo laughed. Then studied Aaron for several long seconds, seeming to realize he was not joking.

"Well, probably easier than it would be for you to get back out... alive."

After some thought, Rengo continued, "There's tight security around the Manor. You would be walking into a den of every imaginable evil. As I mentioned, Lewis Hinton has some type of protection through August. But it's beyond imagination the safeguards or evil deities that reside in the Manor. I know you have the camouflage of a mystic warrior, but you would still be walking into a pit of vipers."

Aaron looked up to Rengo, who was now finishing off his coffee.

"So, do you know how to get in or not?"

Rengo sat his cup on the table, expelled a deep breath and replied, "I do have a clue as to how you might get in. I just wanted to be sure it's what you are determined to do."

Rengo again looked at Aaron, as if giving him one more chance to back away from the idea. He then went on, "August sends his subordinates out to find fresh prey. These lesser vampires are also 'soul suckers,' but they seldom survive long enough to become what might be called real vampires. They are infected victims, just as all the others, ignorant of the fact that their very life force is slowly being drained from them.

They, in turn, feed off others to survive, yet the vampire lord seldom gives one the opportunity to graduate from victim to predator.

"These lesser vampires are sent to parties. They are given bait to hand out to attractive and physically fit persons that might wish to attend a very large party at Sunrise Manor.

"Now, my thought is that you and your girlfriend fall into the category of victims the lesser vampires would be looking for. If you attend some of the larger parties around New Orleans, you might happen upon one of these vampires. And if you make yourself alluring enough, you might just get an invitation to Sunrise Manor.

"You will not likely be noticed by the lesser vampires or other vile deities at the manor, but I suspect August will identify you immediately as being on the side of good. He may not know what you are, but he will most likely sense your positive energy. A purely negative deity such as August will be repulsed by your presence, regardless of camouflage."

Aaron nodded that he understood.

"Thank you for your help."

Rengo chuckled a bit, "You're welcome. But don't feel my assistance is at an end with a bit of conversation. I'm a wealthy man. My wealth is from utilizing positive energy and siding with the creator. I will be available for anything you may need in your struggles. Don't hesitate to ask should you require aid of any kind."

Later that night, after Aaron was dropped off at the warehouse, he went inside and examined the Plymouth closely before moving on to the living area.

As he entered the living room, Sonya stood up from the couch. Suzie jumped down as well and sat down beside Sonya's leg. She then let out a little growl as Sonya crossed her arms and stared at Aaron with anger in her eyes.

"Just where have you been?"

Aaron looked at her and then down to Suzie. His dog let out a disgruntled whine.

"What, you too?" he asked Suzie.

She barked at him.

Sonya began to tap her foot.

"I... well, I was talking to an associate."

"An associate? What did she look like?" Sonya asked.

"It wasn't a she. It was the man at the club, Rengo Winters."

"So, you were partying with that rich guy? How many women were there?"

Aaron began walking toward the bedroom.

"Well, if you call a lengthy conversation concerning the attributes of metaphysical energy or the dynamics of mystical combat a party, then I suppose it was a party. And, there were a few women there. In fact, they waited on us hand and foot. They wore nice, clean uniforms for us as well."

By this time, he had entered the bedroom and was standing at the foot of the bed, unbuttoning his shirt. He turned around, and Sonya jumped into his arms, causing him to fall onto the bed. She immediately began kissing him and taking her clothes off. That was the end of their discussion.

CHAPTER NINE:

Lair of the Vampire

The following morning, Aaron prepared to go out after breakfast. Sonya also got dressed.

"So, where are we going?" she asked as she pulled a blouse over her head.

"We're going shopping. I need you to get some new clothes, makeup, perfume, jewelry… stuff like that. And you can pick me out some clothes as well, while we're at it."

Sonya smiled and moved over to him. She wrapped her arms around his neck and kissed him on the lips.

"I'm not mad at you, Spyder. You don't have to buy me presents… unless you just want to."

Aaron looked down at her sparkling eyes. He considered the situation briefly, then replied, "Uhm, well... just in case, I think I'll get you some things. And they need to be, well, very alluring, not necessarily provocative. And you should get hold of your friends and find out about any celebrations around New Orleans. We're going to be going out to parties. Maybe several a week."

Sonya leaned back and gave him an odd expression.

"Well, if I'd known all this, I would have acted mad at you a long time ago!"

Soon they were busy buying clothes, shoes and fashion accessories. By the end of the day, the Plymouth was full of boxes and bags.

That weekend, the two went to several parties in the area. They moved about and socialized to be noticed. Sonya became slightly intoxicated and was a hit at the gathering, but there was no progress toward getting into Sunrise Manor.

The following week the two attended four parties. Two of them were held in the woodlands with large bonfires burning. These were rather rough in nature as several fights broke out while they were there.

The other two parties were in houses and more civil. Yet, there were no invitations to Sunrise Manor to be had.

As they continued to have no luck making any connections, Aaron began to ask about Sunrise Manor. Sonya quickly volunteered her opinion that it was a seething house of decadence and evil, or so she had heard. Others he spoke with relayed the same sentiments. Though a few mentioned they would like to find out for themselves, most he talked to were apprehensive about visiting the storied residence.

Aaron had a phone installed at the warehouse to stay in contact with Rengo. Sonya became very excited a few days later when they received their first call. She moved quickly to answer it.

As Aaron came from the bathroom with a towel around his waist and another drying his hair, he watched Sonya answer the phone.

"Hello! Who? Well, Spyder may or may not be here. Who wants to know?"

Aaron walked towards her with his hand out. Sonya turned away from him, indicating she was not ready to give up the phone yet.

"Rengo? Rengo who? Are you the guy that kept my boyfriend out all night partying without me?"

Aaron moved around to the front of her and, with a stern face, again held out his hand for the phone. Sonya turned her back to him again.

"Yeah, well, you say he wasn't out partying, but how do I know that? I just find it hard to believe two guys are going to talk that much. Two women maybe, but what can two guys talk about for that long, unless it's about women? And that's what I think was going on, or maybe you two were talking to women, or something more than talking."

At this point Aaron reached around and pulled the phone from her hand.

"Hey, jerk, I was still talking to him! I have a few more questions to ask."

Aaron nodded and then put the phone to his ear.

"Hey, Rengo... Uhm, yeah, she can be a little excitable. But that's not always a bad thing, if you get my drift."

Sonya gave him a sly smile and then went to the bedroom.

"No, we've been to seven or eight parties around New Orleans and a few in the outskirts of town. But nothing regarding getting an invitation to the manor.

"Yeah, well, any leads you get would be appreciated... All right, I'll call you in a day or two."

Aaron hung up the phone. He turned around and found Sonya standing in the bedroom door. She was wearing a pair of black stockings and nothing else. Aaron nodded his head as she smiled seductively. He then went to the bedroom with her.

The following weekend the two were again attending parties. Soon they were in a regular routine of attending every celebration possible. Aaron became focused on the single goal of gaining an invitation to the manor.

With Aaron neglecting his band, it was not long before Bayou Juju began to fall apart. Rick dropped out first. He came by on a Tuesday afternoon. He and Aaron talked in the open warehouse area as Suzie sat beside her master.

"I don't know, Spyder. It's just that you and Sunny are always out partying. We've not been able to set up any gigs, and the band is really uptight. You know, I'm serious about my music. In fact, I'm thinking about going out to California. I've got a buddy out there. That's where we need to go if we ever want to score a contract."

Aaron nodded and pet Suzie as he considered the situation. Rick took another drag from his cigarette and looked at Aaron, as if wanting a response.

"Yeah, I understand, Rick. I'm sorry I've been neglecting the band. It's my fault. You need to do what you feel is best for you. I take full responsibility for the situation."

Rick seemed a little surprised by this.

"Well, you know, Spyder, if you could spend more time with the band, maybe I wouldn't have to split. I mean, we've got a radical sound, and you're a hip bass player."

Aaron shook his head no. "I'm sorry, Rick. I can't do that right now."

Rick stared at Aaron for a few seconds. Then he replied, "Spyder, we can play gigs at parties if you want. I mean, it's like you just want to go to certain parties or something. Every time we play a gig, there's a party. What's the difference?"

"I'm sorry, Rick. I wish there was more I could tell you. But right now, I couldn't say for certain how long it will be before I can focus on the band again."

Rick put his cigarette out in an ashtray by his chair. He nodded.

"Okay, well, that's a real bummer. I'll be by this week to pick up my amp and stuff."

"Yeah, we'll be here. And, stay in touch, Rick. Like I said, it's not you, my friend. It's just something I'm going through right now."

Aaron then stood up, as did Rick. He held out his hand and Rick shook it.

"Yeah, all right, Spyder. We all got to do our own thing sometimes."

Within a few weeks, the other band members had also left to join other groups or start one of their own.

Week after week, Aaron and Sonya attended every social event they could get invited to. Then, around a month after Rick left the band, the phone rang.

Sonya was on the couch watching TV. She jumped up and answered the phone.

Aaron was making himself a sandwich in the kitchen area but turned to watch her.

"Hello. Oh, hi. Listen, I've been thinking." Sonya noticed Aaron watching her, so she turned around and lowered her voice.

"Listen, I've got a girlfriend. She's real cute and loves rich guys. If you could just tell me what really happened that night, I'll introduce you to her."

At this point, Aaron walked up and took the phone.

"Hey, asshole! That's not very nice. I was having a conversation!" Sonya then stormed off to the bedroom as Aaron put the phone to his ear.

"Hey, Rengo. Hmm... Are you sure? Yeah, all right." He turned toward the bedroom door, "Sunny, he wants to talk to you again."

Sonya jumped up from the bed and ran into the living room area. Soon she was back on the phone. She sat on the couch listening, eyes wide, as Aaron ate his sandwich and watched on curiously.

"Really... umhumm, what? Really?" She then began to bite her fingernails. She glanced over at Aaron; her eyes expressed deep concern. She then looked back at the floor and continued. "I... well, no, it's just that, I never thought about that. I mean, I knew... something. Yeah, okay... I will. I promise. Okay, bye."

Sonya stood up and, with an expression of shock mixed with concern, she handed the phone to Aaron. She then marched into the bedroom and shut the door.

Aaron stared at the closed bedroom door for a few seconds, then put the phone up to his ear.

"Just what did you tell her?"

"Oh, I told her you were a secret operative on a highly sensitive and dangerous mission. That anything you do is in the strictest manner to complete your mission and hopefully survive it. I also mentioned that she should simply enjoy the time she has with you because no one can say how long it will last."

Aaron said nothing for a few seconds, then replied, "Oh, I thought you lied to her."

"No, but I feel she still owes me an introduction to her friend, the attractive young woman that loves rich guys."

Aaron chuckled a bit. Rengo continued, "Actually, the reason I called was that I have a very good lead. There's an extremely exclusive party this Saturday evening. I've managed to secure two invitations. You and Sunny should dress, well, let's just say you should be semi-formal, but also exceptionally appealing."

"I understand. Thank you, Rengo. I'll come by tomorrow to pick up the invitations."

After hanging up the phone, Aaron went to the bedroom. Sonya sat on the bed. Suzie had her head in Sonya's lap.

"You all right?" Aaron asked.

She looked at him with sad eyes. Then she stood up and almost jumped into his arms. She wrapped her legs around his waist, and he moved over to the bed, where they fell next to Suzie. The dog moaned as Sonya began kissing Aaron. Suzie then stood and rather reluctantly jumped off the bed as the two made love.

The following Saturday, Aaron had Sonya change clothes three times. As she stepped out the final time in a short skirt and low top, which revealed her neck and ample cleavage, she raised her arms in dismay.

"Well?" she asked, seeming frustrated by Aaron's sudden fashion concerns.

He looked her over. Then walking up close, he examined her exposed neck and upper chest.

"What is this all about? You were always okay with how I dressed before."

Ignoring her question, he said, "This'll work. You should put on some of that expensive perfume."

She looked at him with confusion.

"I was saving that for something really special. It's a very small bottle!"

"You need to put some on tonight. Put plenty on. I'll buy you another bottle."

Sonya expelled a long breath of air, then turned and went back into the bedroom to put the perfume on.

That evening, they pulled up to the elaborate entrance of a large mansion.

A man stepped up to the car as Aaron produced the two invitations. After checking them, the man instructed Aaron where to go.

Once parked, the two walked up the marble steps and into the lavish dwelling. Directly inside the mansion, a man sat playing a large piano. People were drinking and socializing throughout the home as Aaron and Sonya explored one area after another.

In several smaller rooms, there were large tables. People sat around these tables drinking and snorting what Aaron thought to be cocaine.

A waiter came to them and offered two glasses of chilled champagne. They thanked him and, with glass in hand, continued to venture around the large dwelling.

Then, Aaron noticed an attractive young woman. What caught his eye was her hollow and sickly aura as well as a dark blemish on her neck. It would not be visible to others, but Aaron realized this to be a vampire bite.

He motioned to Sonya, and they began to follow the young woman at a distance.

The woman moved purposely through the mass of guests. She scanned the people carefully. Then she stopped in front of a young, well-dressed couple. She spoke with them a few minutes and then handed them each an ornate envelope.

Aaron noticed this appeared to be the last two envelopes the young woman had. As she moved from this couple, Aaron directed Sonya, and they again followed her.

"You got the hots for that chick? Why are we following her?" Sonya whispered.

"Shhh," Aaron said, raising his hand but keeping his eyes on the young woman. Soon she walked up to a small group of people that seemed to be huddling around a table and chairs in the corner of a large room. They all had drinks, and some were smoking.

Aaron noticed all these well-dressed young people had bite marks on their neck. He moved Sonya to an obscure area of the room and watched.

The young woman talked with another attractive woman. As this woman turned and searched through a satchel, the first young woman picked up a drink and downed it. The second woman then handed the young woman a handful of envelopes.

As the young woman began to walk away, Aaron moved in a manner to eventually intercept her. Turning to Sonya as they moved through the mass of people he said, "When she speaks to us, let me do the talking. Got it?"

Sonya struggled in her high heels to keep up with Aaron. She also attempted to hold her champagne upright and not spill it. But she still managed to say, "All right."

After five minutes of careful maneuvering, Aaron and Sonya were directly in the path of the young woman. She walked toward them, examining the guests closely. Then she spotted Sonya, who was by now a bit intoxicated. Her eyes glistened as she took another drink of her champagne and looked around the room with a clueless expression.

"Hi! You look like you're having fun!" the young woman said to Sonya and then, turning to Aaron, smiled.

Aaron smiled back and replied, "We're having a great time. We love these parties. I just wish it had, well, you know, more entertainment. Maybe some poker or, well, I guess I shouldn't complain."

The young woman studied Aaron briefly. Then she looked at Sonya again.

"No, I understand. In fact, you two might be more suited for a party a friend of mine is throwing next Saturday night.

He always has the most exciting entertainment. And there's a huge room for gambling. Plus, dancers and.... well, there's stuff you wouldn't believe."

Again, she looked over the two, but examined Sonya's chest and neck with extra care.

"Are you two interested?" she finally asked.

"Oh, yeah, we're very interested. All of it sounds fantastic. Especially the stuff we wouldn't believe!" Aaron replied with a smile.

"All right. Well, here's two invitations. It'll be at the Sunrise Manor. You'll have to show the invitations to get in."

Sonya almost choked on her drink. Aaron took the envelopes and smiled. As Sonya wiped the excess of champagne from her mouth and looked at Aaron with shock, he gave her a sour glance.

"Thank you," Aaron replied, returning his attention to the woman.

"You're welcome. Have fun!"

She then walked away, again examining the mass of people.

On their way to the car, a somewhat intoxicated Sonya continued to protest.

"I can't believe you're really going to that place!"

Aaron glanced at her and took her arm to keep her from falling, then replied, "Actually, we're going."

Sonya laughed out loud.

"Not me, sweetheart! Haven't you heard about that place? It makes Sodom and Gomorrah look like Disneyland."

She struggled to keep up with Aaron in her high heels, while also balancing her champagne glass but continued, "Spyder, people have gone there and never been seen again! Songs have been written about the place it's so bad. For god's sake, it's a notorious house of evil. Don't you get it?"

He glanced back at her and stopped walking.

"Sunny, I'll protect you. This is something I must do, and I need your help. You told me the day after we met that you wanted to help me. Will you trust me on this?"

She shook her head in an unsure manner. Then she looked at him again, downed the last of her champagne, tossed the glass away and wiped her mouth with the back of her hand.

"I don't want any of those skuzz bags to touch me. Got it? You promise me no one will touch me, and… I guess I'll go… against my better judgment."

Aaron smiled a bit, then replied, "Okay, it's a deal, I promise."

The following Saturday, the two arrived at the edge of New Orleans. The expansive old mansions were spread out in the historic area of the city. Suzie sat in the back seat and let out a whine of unease. Sonya glanced back to her.

"You got that right, Suzie. This whole area is creepy."

They soon pulled alongside Sunrise Manor. Aaron slowed as they crept toward the entrance.

Looking over the large structure and grounds, Sonya spoke with a voice of apprehension, "I heard this place was an old brothel, back during a war sometime. Then someone else said it used to be a women's prison… or nut house. Either way, it's one raunchy place."

Suzie leaned up and licked Sonya's cheek, causing her to giggle and then wipe her face with a, "Suzie, my makeup!"

Pulling up to a weathered and time-worn entryway, Aaron stopped.

A large man that had a dark and withered aura stepped up to the car. As he came closer, his jacket opened slightly, and Aaron noticed a pistol tucked into his belt.

He leaned down and shined a flashlight into the car,

"You got an invite?" the man asked.

Sonya shielded her eyes as the man spent extra time looking her over. Aaron handed him the two envelopes.

After examining the invitations briefly, he handed them back to Aaron and motioned for him to proceed.

Aaron drove the Plymouth to an area used for parking. There were hundreds of cars in what looked to be a vacant field.

Rolling the window down, Aaron glanced to the backseat before getting out.

"Watch the car, Suzie."

She let out a slight bark and then laid down and moved a bit, as if getting comfortable.

The air was heavy and damp as Aaron and Sonya started walking toward the massive structure. From a distance, they could see there were several large bonfires burning at the front of the house. Music was also being played, and as they came closer, Aaron realized it was Bitter Black. He cringed a bit as the vocals again irritated his senses.

After a lengthy stroll, they arrived at the house. There were perhaps a hundred people outside on the porch and front lawn. There were large speakers around the entryway, and they were blaring the music of the fallen angel.

Many guests were either intoxicated or high or possibly both. Several women were walking around in a bikini bottom but no top. Sonya held her hand over Aaron's eyes as one approached and walked past. She then gave him a frustrated expression. He smiled and winked at her as they neared the large building. This caused her to smile as well.

Walking up an elaborately decorated front entry, they moved past several more armed guards. Aaron flashed the invitations, and they were waved inside.

Moving into the building, they observed a variety of people, all busy partying with drugs or alcohol and some were very nearly having sex.

Most of the people had vampire marks on their necks. Many were feeding on each other.

As they ventured further inside, Aaron noticed several women sucking on each other's necks. Sonya looked at them as they passed by. She tipped her head, and her face expressed surprise. Aaron simply smiled and continued to lead her into the house.

Passing by a large open room, they saw all types of gambling: poker tables, roulette and slot machines. Further into the house, there were scantily dressed women dancing on tables as others sat watching. Most were drinking, though a few were obviously doing drugs of some sort.

Cigarette smoke floated all around, and various types of music played in each area. Finally, deep inside the structure, they stopped in a large room, facing an ornate spiral staircase.

As a waiter walked by with glasses of wine, Sonya reached up and took one. Aaron studied the situation and then, seeming to sense something, started walking again.

Before they were across the expansive room, two burly men stepped in front of them. Both displayed vampire bites and auras of severely depleted souls.

Aaron examined the men curiously, and they glanced at him but quickly turned their attention to Sonya, seeming to sense her healthy soul.

"Hello, beautiful," the man on Aaron's right said. Sonya moved closer to Aaron and put her left arm around his waist.

"Excuse us," Aaron said and tried to move around them.

The man that had spoken to Sonya moved to cut off their path, and the two stopped again.

"Shut up, little man!" he said, and his friend laughed about the remark. He then turned his attention to Sonya again.

"Come on, sugar, lose your little boyfriend and let me show you what a real man feels like."

After this, the man reached up as if to take Sonya's arm.

"Don't touch her!" Aaron said in a firm voice that caused the burly man to freeze with his arm in mid air.

He turned to Aaron and smiled, "And what happens if I do touch her, little man?"

Aaron let out a breath of frustration. He turned to the man's friend, but with his right hand, fingers pointed out and stiff, he swiftly struck the arrogant man in his Adam's apple.

It happened so fast Sonya jerked with shock. The man's friend turned and watched his partner grab his throat, eyes wide with pain, gasping for air. Aaron pulled Sonya back a step as the man fell to his knees in front of them, still struggling to breathe.

Aaron looked at the man's friend, as if questioning whether he would make a move. As the injured man laid down completely on the floor, still gasping to breathe, Aaron said to his friend, "You might want to get him some help."

The man nodded with an expression of fear. He then reached down and, pulling the man up to his knees, dragged him out of Aaron and Sonya's path.

Aron took Sonya's arm and again led her toward the stairs. Once they were across the room, Sonya asked, "Is he going to die?"

Aaron replied as they began walking up the spiral staircase, "He's pretty much already dead." He said this referring to the man's soul, but Sonya seemed to take it seriously. Though Aaron didn't notice it, her face winced as she glanced back toward the man now being pulled from the room by his friend.

As they reached the second floor, they passed two people smoking what looked to be a joint. They moved through the cloud of smoke and down a hallway. Soon they came to a set of double doors. Spotting a chair in a nook beside the doors, Aaron directed Sonya to sit down.

"Stay here. Don't talk to anyone unless necessary. I'll be out shortly."

Sonya gave him a face of frustration but sat down, crossed her legs and took another drink of her wine.

Aaron went to the double doors. Taking hold of the two door handles, he paused and lowered his head for a few seconds. Then he opened both doors wide and walked in.

As the doors closed behind him, a large open area presented itself. All around the room were people. Some were having sex while others were smoking or snorting drugs. There were bottles of alcoholic beverages everywhere, and music played softly.

At the other end of the room, elevated slightly from the floor, August sat in a reclining position. There was an attractive woman on each side of him, and he was feeding on one. She held her neck exposed for him as he sucked her living essence. The other young woman rubbed on his chest and seemed eager for him to feed on her.

Everyone in the room had depleted auras, indicating they had been feeding on each other, and then August would ultimately consume the life force, leaving the victims to slowly wither from within.

Aaron had not walked far into the room before August noticed his presence. He looked up from the young woman and stared at Aaron.

The vampire lord appeared to be middle-aged, though Aaron knew he was much older. His hair was jet black, and the hideous image of his vampire state was obvious to Aaron.

Though unseen to his victims, Aaron perceived the aura of a vile demon creature with fangs. It was in the same manner that Aaron perceived Matson's Lycanthrope trait. The image was shadowy across August's face, yet quite visible to Aaron's spiritual perception.

"Essene... What a surprise!" August said. The others now seemed to take notice of Aaron.

"If I had known you were coming, I would have had some milk and cookies prepared." As the vampire said this, his many victims laughed.

Aaron continued to slowly move around the room. He spotted a small shot glass filled with what looked to be whiskey. Reaching down he picked it up and gazed into the amber-colored liquid.

"That won't be necessary. I'm not here on a social visit."

August's face twisted with disgust. But he appeared to buffer up and shouted out, "LEAVE US!"

Immediately everyone in the room began to move toward the doors. Some were half naked and, picking up their clothing, ran out the door.

As the last of the victims ran out, the double doors slammed shut. August reached over to a console beside him. Turning a knob, the music stopped, and the room became silent.

Aaron located a chair and, positioning it directly across the room from August, sat down. He again lifted the small shot glass and peered into the liquid.

"You have a lot of nerve coming here. Or perhaps you're just a fool."

As August said this, Aaron whispered something into the small shot glass. From across the room, it seemed to August that Aaron was smelling the liquid.

"Have you ever heard the saying, 'don't kill the messenger?'"

August's face twisted a bit, as if it were difficult to sit in the same room with Aaron.

"Yes, I've heard it. It means little to me. But if that's why you're here, tell me what Gabriel wishes for me to know and perhaps I'll spare your life."

Aaron again brought the shot glass close to his face, almost touching his lips and again began whispering in Aramaic. As he whispered, the liquid began to glow, ever so slightly. But he held it in such a way that August couldn't see this.

Lowering the small glass, Aaron said, "You should repent, August. While there's still time."

This caused August to laugh in a booming voice.

"You know nothing of time. You live your paltry few decades and then die. I have lived a thousand years. You think just because you're the messenger of Gabriel it means anything to me? Perhaps you feel empowered, but you'll only leave here alive by my grace."

Again, Aaron whispered into the small shot glass. He held it as if he were sipping the liquid, yet as he whispered, the liquid began to glow even more.

August now expressed anguish, as if he had eaten something rotten. His face grimaced and he heaved slightly, as if about to vomit.

"Get away from me. Your very presence disgusts me!" he almost shouted.

"No, I'm not leaving just yet. I have some questions," Aaron replied, then once again lifted the shot glass to his lips and continued whispering to the liquid.

"Has Gabriel sent you here to torment me as well? Leave now, or Gabriel will have one less messenger."

Aaron didn't reply. He continued to whisper into the liquid. He glanced up at August as the vampire began to writhe about uncomfortably in his plush chair.

Finally, after a long moment of silence, Aaron said, "There are questions yet unanswered… and I still have my drink."

With this, August rose to an upright position. His face became strained. Then he shouted, "YOU WILL DIE!"

As if vomiting, he opened his mouth, and a mass of small, black, bat-like creatures came swarming out.

Aaron pulled the glowing shot glass close to him and lowered his head, as if facing a fierce gale.

The horde of bat-like creatures continued to spew from August's mouth. They flew to Aaron and swarmed around him, then completely enveloped him.

When the creatures finally stopped streaming from August's open mouth, there was only a large, black, swarming mass where Aaron sat.

August smiled and laid back into his reclining position. He watched the dark quivering swarm with satisfaction.

Then, he spotted something odd. A glimmer of light shot from the black mass.

August sat back up a little and stared curiously at the swarm.

Suddenly, as a balloon popping, brilliant light burst from the black mass. From outside the room, Sonya was startled by a sudden flash of light from the bottom of the doors. She immediately thought of many flashbulbs going off at the same time. She sat up but remained in her obscure nook.

August raised his hands to his face and fell screaming in pain. The black, bat-like creatures floated lifeless to the floor and disintegrated.

The glow around Aaron slowly began to dissipate as he stood from his chair, but the shot glass in his hand continued to glow brightly as he slowly moved over to August.

The vampire lay on the floor, writhing in pain. His face and hands glowed slightly from the blast of light. As he pulled on his hair in anguish, Aaron could see his eyes also glowed, and he appeared to be blind as he searched the area in a manner indicating he could not see Aaron.

Aaron stood a few feet from the vampire and watched him roll about in agony.

"You'll die for this! You'll pay for this, Essene! I'll kill you slowly and painfully!" August growled.

Aaron walked closer but remained out of reach.

"As I said, I have some questions concerning a young woman by the name of Tori."

"Screw you! I'll tell you nothing. Get out while you can. Run as far as you can. I swear I'll hunt you down and personally destroy you. Do you hear me?"

Aaron stepped closer. He held the small shot glass over August's face. The vampire seemed to be trying to see but was still unaware of Aaron's location.

Tipping the shot glass slightly, one small drop of the glowing liquid fell and landed on the vampire's forehead.

"Aaaaaaggggggggghhhhhhhh!!!" August cried out in pain and rolled around, rubbing his forehead. Then he yelled and held his hands out as the liquid had touched his fingers and they too were glowing.

Outside, Sonya again sat up as she heard the screams. Yet, she remained where Aaron had told her to wait.

Inside, August slowly calmed some but continued to growl in agony.

"That was a single drop, August. I can start dropping it all over you if that's what it takes."

"No, no, wait... I'll tell you; I'll tell you. She's here. He brought her here. I've got her."

Aaron stepped back, looking shocked. He stared at the vampire for several long seconds, seeming unsure of what to do. Finally, he asked, "You have Tori here?"

"Yes, yes, whatever her name is. I don't know and don't care. He just asked me to keep her. You can take her, but he'll rip your flesh off the bones. And you better hope he gets to you before I do, Essene, or you'll wish to die so quickly."

Aaron stood in disbelief. He then asked, "So Lewis asked you to keep her?"

"Are you retarded as well as stupid? Get away from me!" August shouted.

"Where is she?"

"She's in the room downstairs, second door on the left."

"Is the door locked?" Aaron asked.

Reaching into his pocket, August pulled a key ring out with several keys. He tossed them in the direction of Aaron.

"There, now get away from me!" the vampire shouted in anguish.

After picking up the keys, Aaron sat the shot glass of glowing liquid on a small table toward the center of the room.

"I'm moving away from you, August, but I may have more questions."

Aaron then quietly moved to the doors as August moaned in pain.

After slipping out, Aaron thumbed through the keys, finding the one that matched the doors.

As he slipped the key in and turned it to lock the doors, Sonya came to him. He raised his finger and said, "Sshh."

Turning around, there were several of August's women moving toward them.

"August is very upset right now. In fact, he does not want to be disturbed. He said he'll kill anyone that bothers him."

The two women expressed fright. Aaron continued, "You might want to spread the word."

After Aaron told them this, they nodded, turned and left the way they came.

"What's going on?" Sonya asked.

Aaron took her by the arm and led her quickly down the hall and then down the spiral stairs. Soon they were in front of the door August had spoken of.

Thumbing through the keys again, he found several that looked right. As he tried the second key, he could hear August screaming out for assistance.

The third key opened the door. The two entered and found a young woman sitting in a chair. She stared blankly at the wall.

The loud music stopped.

"What are we doing, Spyder?" Sonya asked as he examined the young woman.

Sonya now looked at the woman closely as Aaron seemed very interested in her. She was around nineteen or twenty years old. She had dark-brown hair and was very attractive.

Aaron waved his hand in front of the woman's face. She didn't react to this. He snapped his fingers, and this caused her to look at him, but it was a blank, emotionless expression.

"Come on, help me," Aaron said as he took the young woman's arm.

The woman looked down at Aaron's hand as he took hold of her, but she seemed to be under a spell and moved sluggishly, expressing a complete loss as to where or who she was.

Sonya expelled a breath of frustration as she took the woman's other arm.

"Spyder, you don't need another woman! Am I not enough for you?"

He didn't reply but moved the two out the door. As they more or less carried the woman through the hall, more people and several guards moved toward the upstairs area, where August continued to yell out for assistance.

Out the front door they went and then past the bonfires and people that were now looking around curiously as the loud music had stopped outside as well.

As they hurried and came closer to the Plymouth, Aaron noticed something very odd.

A man was standing with his arm inside the car window. His back was facing them, and Sonya also expressed surprise by the sight.

A few feet from the car, Aaron stopped and let Sonya hold the woman up. He moved around to the front of the man.

"Oh, oh, uhm, hello." The scruffy and unkempt man turned a little. He waved to Aaron and then, looking back also waved to Sonya with his free hand.

Sonya noticed the man had long stringy hair and seemed very nervous.

Aaron investigated the inside of his car and realized that Suzie had the man's other hand in her mouth.

"Well, well, what do you have here, Suzie?" Aaron asked her. The dog moaned, as if glad her master had finally returned.

"Were you trying to steal something from my car?" Aaron asked the man.

"Oh, uhh, no... Aaghhhhh!!" the man shouted as Suzie clamped down on his hand.

Aaron looked the man over again, seeming unsure of what to do.

Expressing bewilderment, along with a loss of patience, Sonya spoke up, "What are you going to do, Spyder? Let's just go, please... just... don't kill anyone else tonight, okay?"

The man's face became stretched and pale with fear. With a trembling voice, he said, "Uh, yeah, Spyder! Please don't kill anyone else tonight!"

Aaron glanced back to the mansion. He could see more movement that was not usual for a party atmosphere.

Glancing at Sonya, he could also see she was eager to leave the area.

Approaching the man, he examined his face in the flickering light of the bonfires.

"I think I've seen you around."

The man nodded a bit, seeming unsure of what to say. Aaron then reached up and put his finger on the man's forehead. The man's eyes moved up and he seemed to go into a trance-like state.

"You stink," Aaron said and then removed the finger.

"Yeah, I'm pretty sure I've seen you before," Aaron said again as the man shook his head, obviously dazed.

"Uhh, huh? Uhm, yeah, yeah, I think I've seen you too, Spyder. Yeah, you remember me, right?" the man replied with a confused expression.

"Okay, you can go. Suzie, let him go." After Aaron said this, his dog released the man's hand.

"What, you just going to let him go? I didn't want you to kill him but letting him go scot free seems a bit lame!" Sonya exclaimed as Aaron went back to help her.

The man quickly jogged toward the mansion, appearing very eager to get away from Aaron.

"Don't worry, he didn't get away scot free." Aaron then helped the young woman into the back seat.

As Aaron drove the Plymouth away from the old structure, the scruffy man Suzie caught trying to steal from the car moved up the steps of the large entryway. He then ventured through the house and on toward the spiral staircase. Standing briefly, he looked up the stairs as there was a commotion going on and the entire house was oddly quiet. There was no music, only people moving around the upstairs area.

Several people standing by the man, grimaced and looking at him, stepped away. The man then moved up the stairs, and as he passed more people, they too waved a hand in front of their face or held their nose.

As he walked toward August's room, he could see the doors open and could hear August. Again, as he passed by people, they moved to get some distance from him.

Inside the large room, the man saw August in his plush chair being assisted by men and women. Though he appeared unharmed, some were trying to use medicine on his skin or around his eyes. He was obviously still not able to see well.

"GET THAT AWAY FROM ME!" he shouted and slapped down some ointment a woman was trying to apply to his skin. "That's useless."

The man watched August but moved around the room. As he did, those around him turned and gave a sour expression or held their nose, waved their hand and stepped away, indicating the man smelled very bad.

Then the man noticed the shot glass that Aaron had placed on the small table. It looked like an ordinary glass of whiskey to him. He glanced around, trying to be discrete.

Then, the man quickly took the glass and moved it toward his mouth. Suddenly, as if the glass of liquid was white-hot, he jerked, and the whiskey spilled on his face, hand and chest. He screamed out in pain and fell to the floor, rolling about as if covered with hot lava.

Everyone's attention turned to the screaming man, they moved away from August and circled around the frightening scene.

Few noticed that August slowly began to laugh. And as the man screamed out in agony, August laughed louder. His hollow eyes lifted, and he laughed loud and hard as the man squirmed on the floor and cried out in pain.

CHAPTER TEN:

Eye of the Needle

The following morning, Aaron, Sonya and Suzie stood in the doorway of the living area at the warehouse. They watched Rengo as he leaned down a few feet from the couch examining the sleeping woman they had brought from August's house.

After turning his head to get a good look at the young woman, he stepped back out, and the four moved into the warehouse to talk.

"He thought that was Tori?" Rengo asked in a hushed voice.

"Well, I don't think he knew her name. It seems he thought I was looking for her when I asked about Tori," Aaron replied.

Sonya stepped closer and spoke in a normal voice.

"Well, why don't you take her with you, Rengo. You can have her. She's very accommodating. She'll go wherever you lead her. I bet she'll do whatever you want her to."

The two men looked at her.

"Uhm, Sunny, could you get us some coffee?" Aaron asked.

She huffed and then marched off toward the living area with Suzie following behind.

Once Sonya had left, the two continued their conversation.

"From the sound of it, the young woman has most likely been mesmerized by August. Do you know if he was feeding on her?"

"She has no bite marks. It seems she was kept in a locked room, likely only receiving food and water."

Rengo rubbed his chin as he thought about this. Then he said, "So Lewis brought her to August. He asked August to keep her. She's obviously a key to something, but what?

"We need to bring her out of her mesmerized state. Vampires use mesmerism to place a person in a docile situation. They can then feed on them until the person is basically soulless. At which point, they can be easily discarded. I've heard of vampires telling their mesmerized victims to go jump off a cliff or to walk back and forth across a busy highway. Seldom does a mesmerized person have the opportunity of being brought out of the state. It will be interesting to see what happens."

After a few seconds of additional thought, Rengo turned to Aaron, "I can't imagine how you managed to get out of August's lair alive. Not to mention bringing her out with you. But I suspect you've not only stirred the hornet's nest up, but fairly well knocked it to the ground and kicked it. You should relocate as soon as possible. I'll take the young woman and bring her out of her clouded state." He paused. "I think I have some garlic."

Aaron gave him a curious expression.

"Yes, garlic. Interestingly, the aroma of garlic will bring a victim from the mesmerized state. It has little effect on vampires. But, considering its effect on mesmerized victims, perhaps they're not very fond of it."

Aaron smiled and nodded.

"Yeah, I agree, August won't remain idle now. I planned on moving to a motel. I'll give you a call once we're settled in."

Rengo nodded, and soon they were escorting the young woman to his limousine.

After breakfast, Aaron had Sonya pack a few clothes and other necessities. By noon they were looking for a decent motel. Once they had found one and got settled in, he called Rengo.

"Hello, Spyder. I'm glad you called. The young woman has recovered. Her name is Naomi Bennett. She was enrolled in an upstate college. When I called, the college said it received a message that she had dropped out of school.

"She says the last thing she remembers was visiting her father. He was astonished and seemed to be disappointed to see her as she had arrived unexpectedly. The next day, she was surprised to get a call from a friend of hers who said she'd recently arrived in town. She'd not seen her friend since high school. The friend asked her to go out and see a new band. It was Bitter Black.

"After the show, her girlfriend from high school took her backstage to meet the band. The lead singer seemed very interested in her. They had a few drinks, and the rest is blank. I'm guessing Lewis slipped her a Mickey and then took her to August for safe keeping."

Aaron considered what Rengo said as he sat on one of the motel room's two beds. Sonya came from the bathroom wearing only a towel. When she noticed Aaron was looking at her, she opened the towel up. Aaron smiled slightly, and this caused Sonya to giggle.

"Are you there, Spyder?" Rengo asked.

Aaron turned from Sonya.

"Yeah, I'm sorry. I was just thinking about what you said." He paused, "So, Naomi's father was disappointed to see her. That sounds odd."

"Well, I did some further investigation on Jerry Bennett, her father. He is originally from northern Louisiana but moved to this area about a year ago. He purchased a small place outside of town. He seemed to be a regular guy, liked to do some farming and such. Then, at some point, her father appears to have mysteriously taken a U-turn.

"His small farm has turned into a haven for drug dealers and all types of undesirables. There's a constant parade of people around his place, and the parties go on 24-7.

"I think Jerry Bennett will surely have some answers for us. I also think having Naomi may give us some leverage if he should not want to answer questions. But we may need to act quickly. August most certainly will."

Aaron considered the situation as he also watched Sonya in the small motel bathroom. After a few seconds, he replied, "Bring Naomi to our motel room." He glanced back at Sonya as she toweled her naked body off. "Give me a couple hours before you bring her over. I'll go talk with her father this afternoon."

There was silence on the other end of the phone. Then Rengo said, "It's very likely he'll have armed guards around

154

the place. If he's aligned himself with Lewis, you may be in for a fight. If not, Lewis will likely have guards in place to keep him there. Either way, you should be cautious."

"All right, I will, thanks." He hung up the phone, and Sonya came from the bathroom and jumped on him.

Later, when Rengo brought Naomi by, Sonya gave Aaron a frustrated stare.

"Uhm, Sonya, this is Naomi.

"Naomi, this is Sonya, but she goes by Sunny."

Naomi smiled and held out her hand. Sonya expelled a breath of frustration but shook her hand.

Rengo gave Aaron directions to Jerry Bennett's place. The two men then observed Naomi and Sonya for several minutes, after which, Rengo left.

Twenty minutes later, Sonya and Naomi were talking and laughing as if they had been friends for years. Aaron sat watching TV, and Suzie lay beside him. When the two women laughed out loud, Suzie glanced at Aaron. He shrugged his shoulders and returned to watching the show.

Around eight o'clock, Aaron pulled a leather jacket from his baggage. He then looked at Suzie. She was on the bed, and the two women were painting her toenails with polish.

"I'm going out. I need Suzie."

Sonya looked up.

"Well, can we go too? Being stuck in this room is a real bummer."

"No, not this time. You two stay here, inside. Don't answer the door if anyone knocks. Keep the curtains closed and the TV turned down. You got it?"

Naomi glanced at Sonya, seeming a bit uneasy by the odd instructions. Sonya nodded and put the small nail polish brush back into the bottle.

"All right, we got it. But don't be gone long."

"Come on, Suzie," Aaron said, and the dog bounced off the bed. Soon the two were driving toward the western outskirts of New Orleans.

Following Rengo's directions, they eventually found their way to a long stretch of dirt road. Several miles later, they came to an expansive two-story house. It was old, perhaps sixty or seventy years old. Around the house were the now-familiar bonfires and multitude of people.

Aaron parked the Plymouth about two blocks from the structure. He and Suzie got out of the car and moved closer.

Music played loudly as Aaron approached and scanned the massive party going on outside the old dwelling. As he looked the area over, he could clearly see several guards on the porch as well as around the house. Pulling a pair of sunglasses from his coat pocket, he put them on and glanced down to Suzie.

"The timing will be tight. We'll have to thread the needle." He looked her in the eyes, and she let out a confirming moan. He then continued, "You've gotten me across worse than this my friend. I'll stay close to you."

Suzie moaned again. She then sat down, seeming to wait for the right moment.

After around five minutes of waiting, Suzie stood up and began to walk toward the house. Aaron followed behind.

Smoke from the fires drifted by them as they came closer to the old home, and the music became louder.

Halfway to their destination, Suzie stopped. Aaron stopped. As they stood in place, a young woman came to them. She appeared to be high on something as well as intoxicated. She offered Aaron a large joint. He smiled and shook his head in a manner indicating he didn't want it. She laughed and moved on. Suzie began walking again. Aaron followed.

As they approached the porch, a guard was distracted by two men fighting. He walked down the steps and toward the commotion as Aaron and Suzie reached the porch. They walked up the steps and went inside.

A thick haze of cigarette smoke and dim lighting greeted the two.

Moving down the hallway, they walked past another guard kneeling down and inserting a hypodermic needle into a man's arm. As the two moved by, the man getting the shot smiled wide, as if the high had just hit him.

Turning the corner, they spotted another guard leaving a room and turning away from them. He had a rifle over his shoulder and walked the opposite direction of Aaron and Suzie.

Suzie approached the door that the guard had come out of. She looked in and then entered. Inside, there was a table and several chairs, a twin-sized bed with crumpled covers and one pillow. A low-grade light bulb hung from a single line and hovered over the table. There was another doorway in the right corner of the room.

Suzie sat down, and Aaron pulled a chair from the table and sat down as well. He noticed a small plate on the table. In the middle of the plate was a pile of white powder. Beside the plate were several short straws and a razorblade.

Aaron picked up the razorblade and began shifting the pile of white powder around. He then chopped it a little as the sound of a toilet flushing was heard behind the doorway in the corner.

A few seconds later, a large man walked from the room and appeared startled to see Aaron sitting at the table. Aaron immediately recognized the man was a mystic warrior as himself, though this man's abilities had obviously declined.

"Who are you?" he asked.

Aaron continued to work the powder around with the razorblade. He glanced up to the man.

"What are you doing, Jerry? Have you become lost?"

Jerry expressed fright. He then seemed to notice Suzie as she sat staring at him.

As Jerry appeared in thought concerning an answer, a guard came to the door. He looked in but obviously didn't see Aaron or Suzie. He then walked on down the hallway.

Jerry swallowed hard. He moved a few steps farther from the bathroom and appeared very nervous. Finally, he asked, "Who sent you? Gabriel?" He paused and then asked, "Michael?" Jerry's voice wavered with fright.

Aaron continued to chop the white powder and move it about. Then he replied, "When one fails a task, there are consequences, Jerry. Often very dire consequences."

Jerry became even more distraught.

"You don't understand. I couldn't even get close. Then they took my daughter. Do you have children?"

Aaron continued to sift and chop the white powder. He glanced up to Jerry but didn't answer him.

After waiting in vain for an answer from Aaron, Jerry continued,

"They'll kill her. They have no compassion. They're unable to forgive or forget. They prey on weakness. You've got to understand."

Aaron glanced over to Suzie. She moaned a bit but continued to watch Jerry.

"A messenger was sent to Lewis," Aaron said.

"Yes, a messenger was sent. A messenger is always sent to give the transgressor an opportunity to turn back. But the messenger simply caused Lewis to become even more cautious. Somehow, he found out I was approaching. He increased his guards. Then he took my daughter, Naomi. If I do anything, he'll kill her. I can't lose her. She's not a part of this."

Aaron expelled a deep breath of air. He sat the razorblade beside the plate.

"Have you forgotten all your training? Everything is connected. Evil will receive justice, either here or on the other side. You cannot decide what or who is a part of this. Only the designs of the creator determine these things."

Jerry hung his head, then shook it with bewilderment.

"I can't risk my daughter. It's too much. I thought I could do it. I can't. I've failed. What can I do?"

Aaron shifted in his chair. Leaning over, he put his arms on his knees and clasped his hands together. He stared at the floor. Again, the guard came by and glanced into the room. Once again, he seemed to not see Aaron or Suzie inside. He then walked on.

"You're at an intersection, Jerry. You must decide which path you'll take. I suggest you repent while there's still time."

Tears came to Jerry's eyes.

"But my daughter. They'll kill her."

Aaron glanced up at him again, "You must decide now, Jerry. There's no more intersections for you and this task beyond here."

Tears began to roll down Jerry's cheeks. Again, he shook his head and then ran his hands through his hair. After pacing back and forth in the small room for several minutes, he turned and walked into the small bathroom. Aaron saw him kneel.

A few moments later, Jerry came from the bathroom, and Aaron knew he had repented. Standing up, Aaron said, "Let's leave this place."

Jerry quickly replied, "There's no way we'll make it out of here alive. And even if we do, if I leave, they'll kill Naomi."

"Have you lost all of your faith?" Aaron asked.

With an expression of fear and guilt, Jerry nodded, "All right."

Aaron glanced at Suzie. She sat for several seconds and then walked out the door with Aaron and Jerry following. She took a different route this time, and they exited the back of the house. After another slow and methodical walk around the large house, they moved on to the Plymouth and left the area.

It was after midnight when they arrived back at the motel. Aaron brought Jerry in, turned the light on and the two women sat up.

"NAOMI!" Jerry shouted.

"Daddy!" Naomi jumped from the bed and immediately hugged her father.

Early the next morning, Aaron was on the phone with Rengo.

"We need to get them out of New Orleans and as far away as possible."

"I agree. I know of a bus station in a little town called St. Rose. It's west of New Orleans. I'll give you directions. Meet me there around 3:30 this afternoon. I'll have the tickets purchased. I'll also give them enough money to get another start."

Aaron agreed, and after jotting down the directions, he went and bought some breakfast.

That afternoon, the Plymouth pulled up to a small bus station in the sleepy little town of St. Rose.

After Rengo gave the information to Aaron, he went over and instructed Jerry, who expressed despair afterwards.

"I don't deserve this. I failed," Jerry said. He glanced at the money and two bus tickets then back to Aaron.

"Failure is simply opportunity from another angle. Life seems unfair at times, but when we're fighting the good fight, we often have a chance to make amends. Perhaps you'll get another chance. It's the difference between good and evil. Good finds new paths and new ways to grow. Evil only knows how to consume what good has produced."

Jerry nodded.

"Thank you, Spyder. I hope I can make amends."

Later, as the bus drove away and Sonya went to the restroom, Rengo spoke with Aaron.

"What about Sunny? The situation is becoming extremely dangerous."

Aaron nodded, "Yeah, I agree. But what to do? She's not going to be safe in New Orleans. Not for a while. I'm at a loss as to what to do with her."

When Aaron said this, Rengo smiled and lifted his eyebrows a bit.

Aaron gave his friend a curious look and then asked, "You got something in mind?"

Rengo replied, "Actually, I do. You may do the heavy lifting in this endeavor, but I like to think I'm the brains. I already foresaw this situation and contacted an associate in Dallas. She does interior design work and will take Sunny on as an assistant. If for some reason Sunny loses interest in that, she'll keep her safe until she's able to return to New Orleans.

"From what I understand, August is beginning to look for you in earnest. I don't think he knows who Sunny is or if he is currently very concerned about her.

"Lewis will also be alerted to the matter after your success in gaining Jerry's freedom. "However, the longer Sunny is with you from here on, the more danger she's in."

Aaron gave Rengo a nod, seeming impressed. "Well, I agree that you're the brains in this partnership. That sounds like a good plan."

The two noticed Sunny walking toward them.

"The problem is getting Sunny to go for it," Aaron said almost under his breath just before she stepped up to them.

The two men studied her briefly. She looked at them both and asked, "Did I miss something?"

CHAPTER ELEVEN:

Waxing Darkness

The following day, Aaron spoke with Sonya. "I've been thinking of a trip. You know, to get away for a while."

Sonya studied him briefly and then smiled, "Great! I think that's a good idea. You know, with all the strange stuff going on, we should go somewhere. And I'm sooo sick of this motel room."

Aaron attempted a smile. "All right, you should pack enough clothes to last a while."

"Well, most of my stuff is at the warehouse," she whined.

"Oh, well, just leave it. We can buy you some new clothes."

Sonya gave him a strange look. "Really, Spyder? I've got clothes I can't replace there. And some jewelry. It'll take five minutes to get it together."

Aaron gave her a look of discomfort.

Sonya pushed his arm. "Don't be so uptight. Loosen up. You're acting like we're Bonnie and Clyde or something."

After some thought, Aaron said, "All right, we'll go in the morning. You'll have five minutes to get your stuff together."

It was almost noon the next day before they made it to the warehouse. Aaron parked a block away.

"Why are you parking here?" Sonya asked.

"I'm just parking here, Sunny. We can walk." Aaron got out and then lifted the seat up for Suzie.

The three walked around a corner and then toward the warehouse. They moved passed a vacant building and a large green sedan parked beside the old structure. They continued along the weathered sidewalk.

Once they reached the door, Aaron looked around cautiously.

"Can you hurry? I need to pee." Sonya then pressed her hand between her legs, as if holding it in.

Aaron unlocked the door and went in first, followed by Suzie and then Sonya.

Before Aaron could look around, Sonya darted toward the living area. Aaron hurried behind to stay close to her.

Moving quickly, she passed the couch and living room area. Aaron moved up behind her as she went into the bathroom.

As he was checking the bathroom, she pulled her skirt up and sat on the toilet. She then shooed Aaron out. Stepping out of the bathroom, Aaron looked around, still feeling apprehensive.

Then he noticed Suzie. She had her head down, sniffing around the living room. Then she began sniffing the couch.

A few seconds later Sonya walked out of the bathroom, pulling her skirt back down.

"Whew, that's a relief. I was about to pop!"

Aaron didn't reply but continued watching as Suzie walked around the couch and looked at the bedroom door.

As Aaron turned and looked at the door, a man stepped out with a pistol. Aaron jumped on Sonya, tackling her in front of the couch just as the man fired. Three shots rang out directly behind Aaron and Sonya as they landed in front of the couch.

Suzie barked and then, jumping across the room, viciously attacked the man. There was a scuffle, then another gunshot.

Aaron heard the man stand and run. Glancing up, he saw the invader move through the door and into the warehouse. Jumping up, Aaron took off after the man. As he moved around the corner, the door to the warehouse slammed shut.

Moving up to the door, Aaron opened it cautiously. As he peeked out, another shot was fired. The bullet hit the building, close to the doorway.

Aaron dodged back behind the door. A few seconds later he carefully glanced out. The large green sedan squealed its tires and came toward the building. It then turned and sped down the street. Aaron stepped out in time to get a look at the license plate.

Closing the door and locking it, he turned around and walked back into the building. Then he heard Sonya crying. Picking up his pace, he moved quickly to the living area.

Stepping in, he saw Sonya by the bedroom door. She was sitting on the floor, holding Suzie in her lap. The dog had been shot, and Sonya's clothes were red with blood. She wept and rocked the dog gently. "Don't die, Suzie! Please don't die! Please don't die!" Sonya mumbled through tears.

Aaron kneeled. Suzie looked up to him. Her eyes were growing dull, and Aaron knew she would not last much longer. A tear welled up in his eye and rolled down his cheek.

Placing her head in his hand, he gazed lovingly into her eyes. "Thank you for saving my life... again."

Suzie moaned, licked Aaron's hand, then her eyes closed for the last time. Sonya continued to weep and hold Suzie. Finally, Aaron and Sonya took her to a small hill overlooking the ocean. It was a place they had taken her when she was a puppy.

As the sun set, they stood looking over the small grave. Sonya still wore her blood-drenched clothes. She wiped a final tear from her eye.

Aaron found an obscure motel at the edge of the city, and the two got cleaned up. As Sonya was in the bath, Aaron called Rengo and asked him to make travel arrangements as soon as possible.

Two days later, they arrived at the same small bus stop in St. Rose that Jerry and Naomi had left from. Aaron carried Sonya's bags but left his in the trunk of the car.

As they stepped into the bus station, Rengo stood with a well-dressed woman in her thirties. Sonya turned and looked at Aaron. Her eyes expressed fright.

"Hello, Sunny. This is Dorothy Edwards."

Sonya nodded to Rengo and shook Dorothy's hand. She then turned to Aaron. He sat her bags down, and she pulled him away from Rengo and Dorothy.

"What's going on?"

Aaron expelled a breath of air. "Dorothy will be traveling with you to Dallas."

Her face twisted. Then he could see tears welling up in her eyes. She looked away and shook her head in disbelief.

"Sunny, I'm sorry. I still have work to do. It's not safe with me."

She sniffed and shook her head, still looking away. Then she looked up to him with tears in her eyes.

"Will I ever see you again?"

"I don't know. I can't say for certain. I'm sorry, I wish I could tell you more."

Her lips tightened, and she wiped a tear from her eye.

Twenty minutes later, Aaron and Rengo stood watching as the bus pulled away from the station.

Once the bus was out of sight, Aaron asked, "You wouldn't happen to have a motorcycle I could use, would you?"

Rengo looked at Aaron.

"No, but you go find what you need and have the seller call me. I'll take care of it."

The following day, Aaron returned to Rengo's house with a new Triumph Bonneville. Inside, Rengo met him in the hallway.

"It's been confirmed. Lewis and Bitter Black have left New Orleans. They didn't tell anyone where they were going. They just disappeared. Everyone thought they might want to take a break, but it seems Lewis decided to move the group somewhere."

"All right, thanks." Aaron then began walking to the room Rengo had let him stay in.

"So, what's the plan?" Rengo asked.

Stopping, Aaron said, "I've got something to take care of. Then we'll check on the plan."

Rengo expressed a lack of understanding but didn't ask anything further.

That evening, Aaron sat parked off the side of a road. He sat on the motorcycle, which was hidden in a wooded area a couple blocks from the entrance of Sunrise Manor.

He stayed in his hidden spot until after midnight. Finally, he pushed the motorcycle out to the road, started it and went back to Rengo's house.

The next evening, he was again in the wooded area beside the road. Again, he waited until after midnight.

On the third night, after ten o'clock, he spotted what he had been waiting for. The large green sedan pulled out from the manor entrance. Turning, it soon passed by Aaron's hidden spot in the trees. He started the Triumph and began tailing the man.

Keeping a distance from the sedan, and at times, turning his lights off, Aaron pursued Suzie's killer far into the country.

Close to eleven o'clock, the man pulled down a dirt road and drove another five miles. Then he turned again and drove for another mile. Aaron followed with his lights turned off. Finally, the man pulled into the driveway of an old house.

Aaron slowed and stopped on the side of the road, then watched from a distance as the man got out of the car, knocked on the door, and then entered.

There were at least ten vehicles parked all around the old structure. There was music playing inside and laughter could be heard as he moved closer to the house.

Easing up to about a block away, Aaron shut off the motorcycle and rolled it behind some trees and bushes. He then crept up to the driveway.

Keeping low, he moved beside the green sedan. Opening the back door, he began to crawl in. His initial intention was to hide in the back seat.

Then, his hand touched something on the floorboard. Taking a closer look, he saw it was a can of oil. He examined it briefly and then thought of a better plan.

Taking the oil, he slipped back out. Moving to the back of the car, he reached underneath and tapped the gas tank to get an idea of how full it was.

Aaron then pulled out a pocketknife and put a hole in the top of the oil can. He then proceeded to pour some of the oil into the gas tank.

Once this was done, he slipped back to where his motorcycle was hidden.

For the next few hours, Aaron sat and dozed. Finally, close to two o'clock in the morning, Aaron noticed the green sedan start up and pull out to the dirt road.

Once the car was past, Aaron started the motorcycle and rode out to the road. He followed at a lengthy distance and with his lights out.

Around three miles from the house, the car began to smoke from the oil in the gas.

Aaron now came closer to the car. He then began to turn his headlight on briefly, then turn it back out.

The sedan began to slow, and it seemed the man had noticed his car was smoking as well as the odd light behind him.

After another mile, the car moved to the side of the road and stopped. Aaron pulled the motorcycle to the side of the road as well. He left the bike running and the headlight on. He put the kickstand down and got off. He then slipped into the woods to his right.

The man walked to the back of his car. He glanced down at the exhaust pipe and the thick smoke coming from it. He then looked back and noticed the single headlight in the distance.

Squinting to see through the thick smoke, he pulled a pistol from his belt.

"WHO'S THERE?" he shouted, then walked a few steps toward the motorcycle.

Lifting the pistol up, he strained to see. Again, he walked toward the light. As he came closer, he could hear the motorcycle running.

"Who's there? I've got a gun! Put your hands up and step this way!"

As the man finished saying this, Aaron came from the side of the road. He stepped behind the man, took the arm that was holding the pistol, pulled it around behind him and jerked it up hard and fast. A popping sound was heard as the man's arm dislocated from the shoulder. The pistol fell from his grasp and landed on the road.

171

"Aagghhhh! What, why the hell did you do that?"

The man stumbled back, but his arm remained in the disjointed position to his side. He leaned over, trying to unlock his injured limb. Aaron stepped in front of him. He then violently kicked the man's right knee, causing it to buckle the opposite direction.

"Owwwww... aaggghhhh..." The man fell to the road; he flopped around in pain. "Please, don't kill me.... agghhhhh, who are you? Why are you doing this?"

The man slithered on the ground, forced to use his left arm and leg.

Aaron took a step forward as the man scooted away from him.

"You killed my dog."

The man shook his head. "I don't know what you're talking about. You've got the wrong person."

"Lying won't help you. It'll just make me angrier." Aaron stepped over and kicked the man's injured leg.

"AAGGGGGGHHH!! Son of a bitch! Oh... shit... agghhh, Okay, okay! I know who you are Yyou're that Spider guy. Listen, I can help you. Please... don't kill me, I'll tell you anything. I can help you. Someone put a price on your head. Someone wants you dead. Listen... I'll help you. I'll help you find out who it was. I'll tell you who my connection is. I'll take you to him. Just don't kill me... I can help you!"

The man continued to scoot toward his car. The thick smoke made him cough. Then he began to cry.

"I just took out your knee. You'll be using a cane the rest of your life," Aaron said as he continued to slowly follow the man.

"What? You're trippin'...aagghhh...what the hell, man? ... Look, it was just a dog."

"No, it wasn't just a dog. And every time you pick up a cane in the morning, every time you use it to walk, I want you to think about my dog. Every day of your miserable life, I want you to remember that dog. And when you get sick of using that cane, I want you to remember what you did to cause your leg to be a wreck."

"You're trippin', man, you're trippin'!" the man yelled and finally reached the side of his car. He then struggled to stand up, using the bumper to help him.

"Shit, aaaooooww oh, son of a bitch... Just... let me go, man. Come on, look, I'll... I'll never bother you again. I promise."

Aaron watched the man as he put forth a great effort and finally got onto his one good leg. The man continued to moan in pain but began to hop toward the open driver's side door.

Stepping in front of him, Aaron said, "Actually, I'm already sure you'll never bother me again."

He then doubled his fist, cocked his arm back and hitting him square in the face, the man fell back on the car and slid to the ground, completely unconscious.

Picking the man up by the collar, he pulled him toward the door and, with some effort, got him in the driver's seat. Aaron then went back and found the pistol. Using a stick to pick the gun up, he tossed it in the passenger seat floorboard.

After this, he used a rag to avoid fingerprints and looked through the car. Finding a bottle of whiskey, he poured some on the man. Then he tossed the bottle in the passenger seat.

Looking under the front seat, he found a cloth bag with an assortment of drugs and paraphernalia. He placed some in the shirt pocket of the man and sat the remainder in the passenger seat, clearly visible.

Finally, he turned the wheel of the car to face a large tree on the right side of the road. He placed the man's broken right leg on the accelerator to throttle the engine up. He then shut the door and reaching into the car, moved the gear shift to drive.

The tires spun, and the car took off. A few seconds later, it slammed into the tree twenty yards away.

The car's engine sputtered and quit running, but the headlights continued to shine into the woods. After waiting a few minutes to make sure there was no fire, Aaron got on his motorcycle and rode back toward New Orleans.

As soon as he found a pay phone, he stopped and called the parish sheriff. He quickly relayed what looked to be an accident and the location of the car, then hung up the phone.

The sun was breaking over the horizon as he pulled up to Rengo's mansion. After getting cleaned up, he went to bed and slept most of the day.

Later that evening, Aaron went downstairs for dinner. As the maid served the meal, Rengo asked, "You're not going out tonight?"

Aaron took a drink of his ginger ale. He looked across the long table at Rengo.

"No."

A silence took over the room for a few seconds. Only the slight metallic sounds from the dishes of food being served was heard. Aaron bowed his head briefly and Rengo did likewise. A few seconds later, Aaron was cutting his steak.

"So, does that mean you've taken care of your business?" Rengo asked.

"Yes," replied Aaron.

Rengo smiled slightly and nodded his head. Nothing else was said.

The following morning, Aaron arrived at the sitting room for breakfast. Rengo sat drinking coffee and reading the newspaper. A maid came in and served Aaron a cup of coffee.

"You can turn the television on if you like, Spyder."

"Oh, no, that's all right. Thanks though."

Rengo glanced past the paper and over to his guest. "Well, I noticed an interesting article in the paper this morning."

Aaron sipped his coffee, then lifted his eyes a bit, expressing interest.

"It seems a man by the name of Owen Puckett wrecked on a country road the other night. When the sheriff found him, his car was loaded with drugs and booze."

Rengo glanced at Aaron, who continued to sip his coffee, while expressing interest in his host.

"The intriguing part is that a gun was found in the car with Owen's fingerprints on it. After some tests, ballistics revealed it was the same gun used in several murders."

Again, Rengo moved the paper aside and glanced at Aaron. Once again Aaron gave no expression but listened intently. Rengo continued, "Now, this next bit is the best part. The authorities felt certain that Owen had done an excessive quantity of hallucinatory drugs due to the fact he claimed, 'The Spider Man' had caused his injuries and made him wreck."

Rengo pulled the paper back once more and looked at Aaron. Slowly a smile broke over his face. Rengo then began to smile as well. Finally, Aaron chuckled, and Rengo laughed also.

After a few seconds, Rengo returned to reading the paper but commented, "I suppose that's what happens when you mix drugs and comic books." Still smiling, Aaron nodded and continued to drink his coffee as the maid rolled a cart in with breakfast.

Later, at lunch, after the servants had left the dining room, Rengo spoke across the table, "I've had no luck finding Lewis and Bitter Black. It seems they've fallen from the face of the earth."

Aaron finished his bite of food. He then took a drink of his ginger ale, sat the glass down and said, "It doesn't matter."

"It doesn't?"

Aaron shook his head, "Nope, it doesn't matter."

Rengo ate a bite of his lunch but glanced over to Aaron. Then he said, "Well, unless you know something I don't, it seems we're at a dead end."

"There's never a dead end in our line of work, my friend. If we don't complete our objective, someone else takes up where we left off."

Rengo took a drink of his wine. "So, is that it for our part?" he asked as he sat the wine glass down.

"I don't know. Do you have a personal library here?"

"Of course. No decent mansion would be without one. In fact, I have one for the public and a hidden one for my alchemist studies. Which would you like to use?"

Aaron glanced over the table to Rengo. "It won't matter. But let's use the one for the public. It might be easier to interpret."

Rengo's face expressed confusion, but he went back to his meal and asked nothing more.

After they had eaten, Rengo took Aaron to the library. He then stood back and watched.

Aaron moved along the shelves of books. He ran his fingers across the binders as he walked. For several minutes, he simply roamed around the large room, running his fingers across the back of the books.

Then he stopped, backed up and, after touching the books one by one, pulled a weathered hardback out. Walking over to Rengo, he opened the book and began to flip the pages rapidly with one hand. Then he stopped around three quarters through the book. Without looking, he stuck his finger on the page.

Handing the book to Rengo, he said, "Put your finger where mine is." Rengo took the book and placed his finger where Aaron's was.

Aaron walked over to a chair and, motioning for Rengo to sit down, they both took a seat. Once they were settled, Aaron continued, "Now, read from where your finger is, and we'll see what comes next."

Rengo studied Aaron curiously but then looked at the book and began reading, "He watched her leave. He didn't turn away until she was out of sight. Then, with a heavy heart, he went back into the house. The next day, he decided he would do a few chores to take his mind off her.

"These tasks helped, but he still felt empty without her presence. He wished he would get a letter or a phone call. A new job would take his mind from the loneliness.

"The following week, he decided to make some of the trinkets that the neighbor children loved so much. As he did this, he felt revived. Time began to go by faster, and then out of the blue it seemed, his phone rang.

"The news was great! It was a job offer. Though not the one he had expected, it had finally come.

"Packing bags and preparing, he briefly considered taking a flight but decided against it as he had plenty of time to reach his destination. He would pack light, travel in leisure and enjoy the scenery."

Rengo turned the page.

"Chapter fifteen."

"That's enough," Aaron said and then stood up.

Rengo looked at the front cover of the book. "Why did you choose this book and this passage?"

Aaron had been staring across the room in thought, but he turned to his host, "Parents can identify their children's voice in the middle of hundreds, and, it works the other way as well. Children can locate their parent's voice among hundreds."

Rengo stood up.

"Hmm, interesting, but still vague. I suppose there are things we're just not meant to understand."

Aaron nodded, "Yeah, that's pretty much it."

CHAPTER TWELVE:

Unfinished Business

The days began to go by slowly and almost painfully for Aaron. Then, a week after reading the book, Aaron found Rengo in the sitting room. "Do you have a writing tablet and pen?"

Rengo was watching television, but he nodded, "Sure, in my office down the hall. Make yourself at home."

An hour later, Rengo peeked into the office. Aaron sat writing at the desk. He then pulled the sheet from the tablet and, setting it aside, began writing again.

Rengo walked in and stepped up to the desk. There was a small stack of papers beside the tablet Aaron was writing on.

After picking one up and reading it, he looked at Aaron. For another minute, Aaron continued to write. He then pulled the sheet from the tablet and sat it with the others.

Finally, he gave Rengo his attention.

"This is really good, Spyder. I didn't realize you were a poet."

Aaron gave him an odd expression, "I didn't realize it either. They're songs. They just started coming to me, and I had to write them down."

Rengo picked another one up, "Do you know why?"

"I have no idea," Aaron replied.

After looking over the other paper he'd picked up, Rengo said, "You should get a copyright on these."

Aaron shook his head, "I'm not worried about that; I don't have time."

He then began to write again.

"Well, I'll make a deal with you. I'll have them typed up and will obtain a copyright on them. If anything comes of it, we can split fifty-fifty."

Aaron seemed to barely hear what Rengo said, but he nodded, "Yeah, that's fine, if you want to take the time." Rengo gathered the papers up and left as Aaron continued to write.

On and off for a week straight Aaron wrote songs. Rengo would take them and have the lyrics typed up in preparation for a copyright. He then returned the handwritten copies to Aaron.

After a week, Aaron suddenly had no more inspiration to write. He sat drinking coffee with Rengo before breakfast.

"That's really unusual. You write lyrics for hours at a time, day after day for a week. Then you wake up one morning and nothing?

Aaron nodded and sipped his coffee. A servant rolled the breakfast cart in. Both men stood and began preparing a plate.

Once they had sat down, Rengo asked, "So, we just continue to wait?"

Aaron spread some butter on a slice of toast.

"I'm thinking the songs were the 'trinkets which the neighbor children loved so much.' So, now we're waiting for something 'out of the blue' to happen."

Two days later, Aaron and Rengo were playing a game of pool in the recreation room when a maid walked in.

"Sir, you have a call."

Rengo sat his pool cue down and, walking over to a phone, picked the receiver up.

"This is Rengo Winters."

His face twisted slightly, and he looked over to Aaron. "I'm sorry, who is this again? Oh, I see, well, yes, I do happen to know of Spyder's whereabouts. In fact, he's right here. Would you like to speak with him?"

Aaron straightened up from a position of making a pool shot. He leaned his pool cue on the table and walked over to the phone. "Hello?"

"Hey, Spyder! It's Rick! Man, this is outta sight! I can't believe I found you! Everyone says you and Sunny just disappeared, and the warehouse is empty now."

"Oh, yeah, it's kind of a long story. But it's sure good to hear from you, Rick."

"Man, I'd about given up on finding you, Spyder. Then I came across old Rengo Winters' business card. I forgot I even had it. I thought, well, maybe it's worth a shot! I never imagined I'd be talking with you so soon!"

Aaron looked over to Rengo. He shrugged his shoulders, and Rengo raised his eyebrows in a puzzled manner.

"Yeah, it's great to talk with you, Rick. Uhm, how have you been?"

"Great, Spyder! Listen, the reason I've been trying to get hold of you is I'm out here in Los Angeles, and we've got this dynamite band together. It's really getting tight and all. But we need a bass player. I told the guys about you, and they're all psyched about it. I'm hoping you're back into playing. This is a real shot, Spyder. I feel like this band can hit it big if we can get the right people together. What do you say?"

Aaron didn't say anything for a few seconds.

"You still there, Spyder?"

"Yeah, yeah, I'm still here, Rick. You know, I think you called at just the right time, my friend. In fact, I've been hoping something would come up. I've just been hanging around, doing nothing."

"Oh, dude, that's far-out! Hey, bring Sunny too. She'll get along super with the other girls!"

"Oh, well, Sunny and I are no longer together."

"Ahhh, oh, I see. Yeah, well, that's a real bummer. I see why you've been hoping for something to come along. Well, don't worry. The chicks out here are dynamite. And you'll get her off your mind as soon as you start playing again.

"But get out here as quick as you can. I'll give you the address to our studio. It's an old store building, but we've got it set up real boss. You got a pen and paper?"

"Yeah, hold on just a second. I'll get a pen and something to write on."

A few minutes later, Aaron looked over the directions as he hung up the phone. Rengo shook his head in disbelief. "That's amazing, out of the blue."

Aaron smiled as he folded the address, "Out of the blue."

Later that day, as the two were being served dinner, Aaron said, "I'd like to take the motorcycle to California."

Rengo replied, "You can take it, it's yours. I'll have the title changed right away."

"No, I appreciate it, but I don't feel right just taking it. I'll trade the Plymouth for it."

Rengo considered this. "That's not a fair trade, Spyder. But I respect your reluctance of taking it for free."

He thought about it for a few more seconds. "I'll tell you what. If you want, I'll have both our names put on the two titles. This way we can keep the plates up to date and such. When you get back this way, we can swap back. How does that sound?"

Aaron was chewing a bite of food. He examined his plate as he thought of Rengo's suggestion. Then he replied, "That sounds fine to me. I'll call and give you my address once I get settled."

They continued to eat their meal. Afterwards, Rengo asked, "So when are you planning to leave?"

"I'm not sure. I'll get packed up tomorrow. Since I'm taking the bike, I may leave the day after. It'll take a while on the motorcycle, but it seems I have plenty of time to enjoy the scenery."

Rengo stood from the table. He walked over to Aaron, and reaching up, he took Tori's crucifix necklace off.

"Here, I truly feel Tori would like for you to take this."

Aaron looked at the necklace in Rengo's hand, then looked up to him, "Are you sure?"

"If I wasn't sure, there's no way I would give it up. I really feel I should send it with you and that you should wear it, perhaps in honor of her. I don't know; I don't have the same abilities that she had or that you have, but I sense I should send it with you."

Taking the necklace from Rengo's hand, Aaron began to put it around his neck.

"If that's how you feel Rengo, I'm certain it's right." The two men smiled and went to the recreation room for a game of pool.

Two days later, Aaron said goodbye to Rengo. Then, after a brief stop at Suzie's grave, he began his journey to California.

Progress was slow on the motorcycle. Ten days later, he was over halfway. When he finally reached Arizona, the pace quickened.

Two and a half weeks after leaving New Orleans, Aaron pulled up to the old store building that Rick's band was using for a studio. The sound of rock and roll permeated the walls of the old structure. Taking the duffle bag from his back, he carried it into the makeshift studio.

Directly inside, several people sat on large couches. They were smoking cigarettes and various illegal substances. Several of the women eyed him as he passed by, following the music.

Through another door, he found a short hallway. The band could be heard past the wall at the end.

A large man with long hair sat in a chair at the end of the hall. He was watching the band but stood and walked toward Aaron. "Hold up. Who are you and what's your business?"

"I'm a friend of Rick's," Aaron replied.

The man looked at him suspiciously but nodded for him to follow.

Before reaching the end of the hall and seeing the band, Aaron could clearly hear a bass player. As he rounded the corner, he could see a five-piece band. Rick was on lead guitar. Behind the band was a large, hand-painted tapestry with the name 'Midnight Drifter' written stylishly against a dark background. Aaron concluded this must be the band's name.

A long-haired, slender singer was positioned in the middle of the small stage, moving around in a carefree manner, seeming to practice his act.

The drummer had a large and elaborate set of percussion instruments, including a nine-piece drum kit. To the right of the singer, a bass player and rhythm guitarist were looking at each other. It seemed they were working on the foundation of the song.

As soon as Rick noticed Aaron, he smiled and nodded. The man led him to an area where several young, attractive women sat. Most smoked cigarettes and one was drinking a beer.

The man leaned over and spoke close to Aaron's ear, "You can wait here."

Aaron nodded rather than attempting to speak over the loud music. He sat down and watched the band.

As the song entered the chorus, the singer began to sing, but it seemed to be random words. He would do more moaning and wailing than actual singing. He then moved around and again seemed to be practicing his stage act.

As the song ended, Aaron felt the group was tight, but obviously in need of actual lyrics.

"Spyder! Hey, you made it!" Rick almost shouted as he took off his guitar and sat it in a stand.

Aaron waved. Rick jumped down from the stage and was soon shaking Aaron's hand.

"Hey, guys, this is Spyder!"

As Rick said this, Aaron noticed the bass player appeared concerned. The other members of the band stepped down and were soon shaking his hand as well. The bass player was the last to do so.

"Man, I thought you would be here sooner than this." Rick then fidgeted a bit and continued, "I called Rengo the other day. He, uhm, well, he said you had left a couple weeks ago, and he didn't know where you were."

Aaron nodded, "Yeah, it took me a bit longer because I rode my bike out and ran into some bad weather along the way."

"Ahhh, yeah... well, uhm…," Rick turned and glanced back at the others.

Then the bass player spoke up, "Hey, uhm, I need to go check on Cindy. I think she was needing some smokes."

"Yeah, all right, Jake," Rick said.

After he was gone, the singer, whose name turned out to be Terry, looked at the girls on the couch. "You chicks leave us a while."

The girls stood up and, after adjusting their short skirts back down, left the studio as well.

The band sat down, and Rick sat across from Aaron. "Uhm, well, I guess you saw we have a bass player." He paused and rubbed the back of his head, seeming nervous.

"We just kind of came across Jake. I really thought you would be here sooner, Spyder. Everyone has taken a shine to Jake, and well, he's fitting in really well."

Aaron nodded, "That's all right, Rick. I should have got here sooner."

"Yeah, well, we just hired Jake a few days ago. I mean, if you would have made it a few days sooner. I really hate that you came all the way out here for nothing."

Terry lit up a cigarette and expelled a long stream of smoke, "I'm sure you can score a band out here, Spyder. We'll help you."

"Sure, there's a lot of hip bands around," the rhythm guitarist said. "Maybe you could help us out in the meantime. We could always use another roadie. It would just be until you find a band of your own."

Terry broke in, "Yeah, sure. We always need help with the equipment. We can't pay a lot of bread, but we can feed you and you can crash in the studio."

The others nodded, and Rick watched his friend, seeming interested in his thoughts.

"Yeah, that sounds groovy," Aaron replied.

Everyone smiled and seemed to relax.

"So, what did you think? Did you dig the song?" Rick asked.

Aaron thought a few seconds before answering. "Yeah, the music is tight and hip. I couldn't really catch the lyrics though."

Terry sat up, in a seemingly defensive posture, "Oh, yeah, man. That's just some stuff I was laying out there until we get the tune together."

Aaron nodded, "Cool. Well, the music was rockin'." He paused, "You guys needing some lyrics? I got some stuff I put together a while back."

Rick glanced at Terry, "Uhm, Terry writes our lyrics. He's got some hip stuff."

The drummer, who had said little, spoke up, "Let's see what Spyder's got. Terry's got his hands full right now."

The rhythm guitarist laughed, "Yeah, his hands full of Alice."

The others laughed, and Terry blew out another long stream of cigarette smoke. "Get real, guys. You just wish your girls were as hot as Alice." He then turned to Aaron. "Let's see what you've got, Spyder. It can't hurt to look."

Aaron opened his duffle bag and pulled out a battered folder. He then fished out several sheets of tablet paper and handed them around to the band.

Silence held the large room as everyone looked over the lyrics. Terry pulled one last drag from his cigarette, crushed it out in an ashtray, then quickly looked back to the paper.

Nodding and offering his sheet, the rhythm guitarist traded his paper with the drummer's, and both again examined their new lyrics. Likewise, the other band members swapped their sheets.

"I've got more here, if you'd like to see them," Aaron said.

Terry glanced around at the other band members and then turned his attention to Aaron, "You've got more? How many?"

"Oh, around sixty-something," Aaron replied.

"These are, uhm, not bad, Spyder."

"Not bad?" the drummer asked, seeming disappointed with Terry's assessment.

"Yeah, well, they're kinda rad. But we need to check them out first," Terry said, giving the drummer a look, as if to quiet him.

"Kind of rad? You're trippin'. They're totally righteous," the drummer replied under his breath as Terry stood up.

"Let's try this one with the tune we've been calling number eight," the singer waved the sheet of paper in his hand. "Bring the girls back in, and we'll see what they think," he added as he stepped up on the stage.

Once their girlfriends were back in the studio and sitting down, the band erupted in a lively rock melody.

Holding the sheet of paper up, Terry began singing Aaron's lyrics. Immediately the band's girlfriends took notice. By the time the song was over, the girls, along with the small group from the front, were all standing around the stage, waving their arms and cheering.

Inspired by the reaction, the band tried another set of lyrics to music they had put together. It also energized the girlfriends and fans from the front.

From this point on, the band began to use Aaron's lyrics. He was hired as a roadie and offered a place to stay in the studio. He decided to locate a small apartment instead.

After the agreement had been reached, Aaron left the studio to search for a hotel to stay the night. Rick came out and caught him just before he kick-started the Triumph.

"Hey, Spyder! Dude, I didn't know you wrote songs. You should have been writing for Bayou Juju. We may have already scored a contract."

Aaron smiled, "Thanks, Rick. I haven't been writing for long. They just sort of came to me a while back."

"Well, we're all digging it, man. I think Terry is a little jealous, but your songs are badass righteous."

"Thanks," Aaron then kicked the starter on the bike and gave it a little gas once it was running.

"Hey, you sure you don't need a place to stay. You're welcome to crash at my pad until you get a place."

"Oh, I'll be all right. I can stay at a hotel a few days until I get an apartment. I'll keep your offer in mind though."

With that, Aaron went to a hotel. The next morning, he found a small, furnished apartment, rented it, then went to the studio.

There was an obvious excitement in the air as the band began putting more of Aaron's songs to Midnight Drifter's music.

Within three weeks, the band had decided to increase the amount of shows they played. Aaron worked with the equipment but otherwise tended to stay in the shadows. He would tune the guitars and repair chords. The pay he received was not enough to live on, but he still received a disability check from his time in the army, so he didn't complain about the pay.

Within a couple months of Aaron's arrival, the band was playing three to four shows a week, as opposed to their previous schedule of two or three shows a month.

It was during one of these shows, in the heart of Los Angeles, that Aaron came across his adversary. As the band began unloading their equipment from the van, Rick yelled out to Aaron, "Hey, Spyder, get a load of this!"

Aaron was carrying several guitar cases to the backstage area of a large club. He sat them down and came over to where Rick was standing.

"Look, it's that band Bitter Black. They're playing here tonight after us."

Aaron examined Bitter Black's poster next to Midnight Drifter's.

"They're from our neck of the woods. You remember those guys? I never met them personally, but they played all around New Orleans while we had Bayou Juju going."

"Yeah, I remember hearing about them. I haven't met them either, but I do recall them playing around New Orleans," Aaron replied.

"Maybe we can talk with them tonight. I'll bet they would like to talk with some dudes from their hometown."

Aaron glanced at Rick, "Ahh, you go ahead if you want. If you recall, I'm actually from Kansas."

"Oh, yeah, well, I might say hi. Their music is way harder than ours anyway. And, from what I've heard, they're kind of freaky. I just thought you might want to talk with them."

"Well, like you said, I doubt they're into Midnight Drifter's style of music. I'm guessing they have their own crowd."

Rick nodded, and Aaron went back to unloading the van.

Soon after this, Bitter Black's van pulled up to the back of the club. Behind this came a large station wagon. As the band members exited the car, Aaron knew Lewis on sight.

The man was of medium- build. For the most part, he had an ordinary appearance. He had long hair that looked to have been colored black. He was clean shaven and wore sunglasses.

But Aaron could clearly see the aura of a fallen angel. It was the first of this kind he had seen possessing a human. The face was beautiful, yet dark and forlorn in expression.

Lewis looked around and Aaron glanced down at the bundle of wires he was rewinding. Once Lewis had looked away, Aaron went back into the club and stayed in the shadows.

That night, it was a packed house as the bands raised the already high level of excitement. The first band to play was not bad but obviously lacked material and polishing.

Once this band was off the stage, Aaron and several other roadies quickly set up Midnight Drifter's equipment behind a closed curtain.

As Midnight Drifter performed its show to an enthusiastic crowd, Aaron watched Lewis from behind the stage. The singer sat with the band and their female companions.

It was obvious the fallen angel possessing Lewis' body had become very attached to the physical realm. He was treated like royalty by the mortals due to unearthly charisma emanating around him.

An hour and a half later, Midnight Drifter wrapped their set up. Aaron assisted the other roadies as they removed the band's gear and equipment from the stage. Meanwhile, Bitter Black's crew worked to set up their band's equipment.

Once Aaron and the other roadies had loaded the van, they went into the club to watch Bitter Black.

As the group began to play, there was an immediate reaction by the crowd. Lewis' vocals were strong and aggressive. Though no one else could see it, Aaron could clearly visualize the spiritual resonance expelling from Lewis' mouth. It was affecting the mortals like a drug. They became thrilled and excited by the fallen one's voice and song.

Aaron remained in the shadows. He sensed the lure of the angel's words, enticing all those listening to follow him down a dark path, but Aaron remained steadfast.

The members of Midnight Drifter quickly became intoxicated by the songs of the fallen angel. The entire band was acting like fans by the time Bitter Black's set was over.

Once the band was off the stage, Aaron noticed Rick talking with Lewis, apparently telling him they were both from New Orleans. Lewis acted casually interested but soon brushed Rick and the other admirers off. He then went out the back door, loaded into the station wagon with the other band members and left.

On the way back to their studio, everyone, except Aaron, spoke enthusiastically about Bitter Black's performance.

"Terry, can you get a little more edge to your vocals?" the drummer asked from the back of the van.

Sitting in the front seat, Terry turned back. With reflections of streetlights moving across his face, he shouted, "Shut up, Bo."

Bo laughed at this and continued to twirl his drumsticks.

Rick then spoke up, "You know, we should get a little harder though. Did you see Bitter Black's fans? Dude, that was a tight set. They were smokin'."

"Look, if you guys want me to be Lewis Hinton, why don't you just go ask him to join Midnight Drifter instead!"

The band members chuckled about this. Then Rick replied, "Come on, Terry. We don't want another singer. But you must admit, they've got a groovy gig. Didn't you dig it?"

"Yeah, I can dig their set and maybe we can get a little harder, but I'm not going to be anyone but me. Can you guys dig that?"

Again, everyone laughed. Then Rick glanced back and noticed Aaron sitting quietly in the corner of the van.

"What do you think, Spyder? We should be more like Bitter Black, don't ya think?"

Everyone turned to Aaron. Light from the passing streetlights barely lit up his face. For several long seconds, he said nothing. Finally, he answered, "Lewis is leading his followers to a place he knows well. It's the same place he named the band after." He paused briefly and then added, "Terry's right. We should be who we really are. Which is not what Lewis Hinton is doing."

Terry immediately reacted with a "Hell yeah! You see there? Spyder digs what I'm talking about!"

The rest of the band let out a moan of disappointment. A few minutes later they pulled up to the makeshift studio.

The following day, Aaron went to a bookstore and purchased a Bible. Back at his apartment, he thumbed through the New Testament until locating a specific verse. The words were in red. He carefully removed the page from the book, then folded it and placed it, along with a straight pin, in his wallet.

***

As their popularity grew, Midnight Drifter crossed paths with Bitter Black again and again. Though Midnight Drifter always opened for the more popular Bitter Black, both were gaining momentum in the LA club scene.

Four months after they first opened for Bitter Black, Midnight Drifter again found itself performing prior to Lewis' band.

Aaron worked to set up Midnight Drifter's equipment as Lewis and Bitter Black entered the back door of the club. As usual, a large entourage surrounded the singer.

From a corner of the stage, Aaron studied Lewis. The singer lit up a cigarette, then reached over and pulled the curvy blonde next to him closer. She giggled and caressed his chest as Lewis looked the area over, then moved toward the front of the club.

That evening it was once again a packed house. Between the two popular bands' followers, the building was almost at standing-room-only capacity.

From the shadow areas backstage, Aaron watched as Midnight Drifter and then Bitter Black rocked the house.

Before the final song by Bitter Black, Lewis made an announcement to the crowd, "Thank you! I've got the lowdown for all our fans. For anyone here that's not our fan, you can kiss my ass!"

The crowd laughed, and more than a few young women shouted a desire to do so. Lewis continued, "Bitter Black is in negotiations for a contract with Capstone records! Once I sign the deal, we'll take over America! Then... the world!"

The crowd went wild, and the band immediately started in on one of their most popular songs. Lewis again belted out the lyrics with his aggressive voice.

Later, the singer came backstage with a beer in one hand and the curvy blonde under his other arm. "Hey, you guys laid down some hip jams tonight!" Lewis almost shouted as Midnight Drifter helped their roadies with the gear. He then continued, "You're all invited to a party we're having to celebrate my... our new contract. My crew can give you the address. Be warned though, it's a Bitter Black party, so it will be a decadent violation of all that is good!" He then laughed and moved toward the backstage exit.

Once Midnight Drifter had loaded their equipment, they eagerly headed toward the upscale Beverly Hills neighborhood where the party would be held.

Twenty minutes later, the van turned into the drive of a large and luxurious mansion. Stopping at the gate, a guard shined a flashlight into the interior.

"We're Midnight Drifter. Lewis invited us," Rick said from the driver's seat.

The man studied Rick briefly and then, after a look around the van with the flashlight, waved them on.

As they approached the large dwelling, lights outside and inside lit the house up.

"Man, this is outta sight! I wish we had a pad like this!" Rick exclaimed as he parked.

"It's probably just one of the fan's houses. Bitter Black might have this kind of bread after they sign the contract, but I doubt they do now," Terry replied sarcastically.

The group climbed out of the van, and Aaron followed them into the house. Music could be heard long before they stepped in. A woman laughed and ran out past them and down the steps. A few seconds later, a long-haired man, dressed only in underwear ran past in pursuit of the woman.

"Whooohooo!! Now this is what I call a party!" Bo yelled out.

Soon the band and crew were drinking and mingling. Aaron held a beer in his hand but watched Lewis from a distance.

Around 2:30 in the morning, Lewis and his girlfriend moved from the party, down a hallway and to a room. Aaron followed, careful to remain unseen.

Moving inside the room, Lewis hung a 'Do Not Disturb' sign on the knob and slipped back inside.

Aaron waited a few minutes and moved toward the room. Passing by a small table, he spotted a pair of drumsticks. He picked them up and proceeded to the door.

Turning the doorknob, the lock clicked open for him, and Aaron quietly stepped inside. Once in, he re-locked the door.

Around the short-walled entryway, Aaron could hear Lewis and his girlfriend. They were in the process of having sex. Aaron could hear the woman moan.

He reached back and pulled out his wallet. Locating the folded page, he'd removed from the Bible, he unfolded it, took the straight pin out and hung the page on the door, around eye level.

Once this was done, he took the drumsticks and began to whisper a phrase in Aramaic. Over and over he whispered the ancient phrase until the sticks began to glow ever so slightly.

Aaron then walked around the entryway wall, where he saw Lewis on the bed, wearing only a pair of jeans and leaning over his half-clothed girlfriend. He was kissing her and caressing her, but as soon as Aaron entered the room, she fell asleep.

"Hey, bitch, you can't pass out on me now!" Lewis said with dismay.

Aaron moved around Lewis as he inspected his limp girlfriend. Then, when Aaron had moved to the side of the bed, around ten feet from Lewis, the singer suddenly noticed him.

"What the hell are you doing here, asshole? Can't you read? The sign says do not disturb!"

Aaron studied the singer and said nothing. Lewis climbed off the bed and faced him, "What kind of shit-for-brains are you? Get out of here before I rip your head off!"

Aaron asked in a calm voice, "What's your name?"

Lewis appeared to be barely restraining himself, but he answered, "I'm going to pull your head off and shit in it!"

Aaron began to twirl one of the drumsticks. He held the other in his hand as if it were the handle of a shield.

"I wish to know who I am speaking with. The one that has taken possession of a mortal's body."

Lewis suddenly realized Aaron was not a trespasser. His expression changed yet remained twisted with anger. Glancing at the glowing drumsticks, he replied, "Are you shitting me? Another messenger? How many messengers is Gabriel willing to sacrifice?"

"What's your name?" Aaron asked again.

"My name is Locsheen... mortal." With this, the fallen angel's real features became clearer. Aaron could see that Locsheen was both beautiful and evil.

Aaron took a step to the side but continued to twirl the glowing drumstick while watching Locsheen closely.

"Now, deliver the message. and perhaps I'll make your death quick and a little less painful than the last messenger," the fallen angel said.

Aaron replied in an assertive but monotone voice. "Locsheen, you've been warned to withdraw from the physical realm and the mortal body you've taken over. You know well the laws set forth from the beginning by the creator. Thus, you will receive judgment for your transgressions." Aaron began to twirl the stick faster, and both sticks began to glow brighter. He then said in an assertive voice, "The message is death."

Locsheen's face became enraged, and the full view of his form radiated around Lewis' body. He spread his arms, revealing large claws and shadowy red wings. Then with a growl of anger, Locsheen attacked.

One of Aaron's drumsticks became as a sword of light. He raised the other stick in a defensive position, and it became as a shield of light. Yet the power of Locsheen's attack threw Aaron against the wall, and he barely remained on his feet.

Locsheen pressed hard against Aaron as he held the light shield up to defend himself. The fallen one screeched out in anger and attempted to bite Aaron. The ferocity was like an attack dog chomping to get a piece of Aaron's face. Ducking down behind the shield and using the wall as leverage, Aaron pushed hard and forced the fallen angel back. Immediately, Aaron swung the sword and inflicted a gash on Locsheen's forearm. A horrid screech of pain came from the fallen angel.

In the large house, music and mayhem from the party drowned out the epic struggle inside the room. Only flashes of light under the doorway belayed the spiritual conflict within the bedroom. It was a ferocious and violent struggle.

Again, and again the two advanced upon each other, trading wounds. The room looked as if it was hit by a hurricane. Still, Lewis' girlfriend slept, never rousing to the chaos all around her.

Aaron fought Locsheen for what felt like hours. He was battered and weary. Locsheen had also been badly wounded. He crawled to the door, seeming to want to escape the fight. His breathing was labored and raspy from a gouge of the light sword to his chest.

Slumping over and leaning on his knees, Aaron watched Locsheen stand and move around the entryway. As soon as Locsheen reached for the doorknob, the red letters on the page became as fire, and the power from the words forced Locsheen to stumble back in pain.

"Aaaghhhh, you... pathetic mortal! YOU CANNOT DEFEAT ME!" he shouted in anger, and then lunged toward Aaron, who wearily raised his weapons of light in defense.

Again, the two battled in the small bedroom. Outside the room, Bitter Black's guitar player guzzled down a beer. The drummer had his face in the cleavage of a buxom fan. The bass player was passed out in a large chair. The music blared, and partiers danced about as someone flashed the lights on and off.

In the now-destroyed room, Locsheen gasped for air. Aaron was on his knees, also struggling to breath. His head drooped from exhaustion, but he kept his eyes focused on the injured angel.

Locsheen's eyes were red with rage, and he held his chest in pain. "Who are you? You're not a messenger. You're not immortal. Who the hell are you?"

Aaron continued to stare at the fallen angel. He knew he could not go on much longer. He was spent and could barely hold himself up.

"WHO THE HELL ARE YOU! I DEMAND YOU TELL ME!"

Then inspiration came to Aaron. Yet he knew he would only have one chance. He struggled to his feet and said wearily, "I'm the pathetic mortal that will destroy the great 'Locsheen.' That's who I am. And that's what you will have to tell your associates in hell."

Locsheen's face grew fierce as anger welled inside him. Aaron steadied himself and placed his feet where he needed them to be. The fallen angel spread his long arms, stretched out his claws and flung himself at Aaron.

At the last second, Aaron dropped, rolled to the side and swung the light sword at Locsheen's leg.

A scream of pain rang out, filling the small room. Aaron staggered to his feet and looked back.

Though the leg of Lewis was still intact, the leg of Locsheen had been severed from the angel's body, and the fallen one lay on the floor in agony.

Aaron stepped a little closer as Locsheen growled and writhed about in pain.

Facing the injured being, Aaron knew he was about to collapse. They stared at each other. Aaron teetered on his feet. The fallen angel almost smiled now, seeming to understand Aaron had no more energy.

With the last of his strength, Aaron stepped forward and swiftly thrust the light sword into the fallen angel's face and head. As Aaron stumbled back and fell to the floor unconscious, the last thing he heard was an unearthly howling of pain and rage.

Aaron woke about an hour later and found himself staring at the ceiling of the room. He struggled to pick himself up from the carpet. Lewis lay motionless on the floor about eight feet away.

Laboring to breathe, Aaron staggered toward the door. Leaning on the doorway, he pulled the page from it and tossed the pin aside. Still struggling to pull air into his lungs and holding his chest in pain, Aaron opened the door.

Stumbling through the house, he passed by a now less raucous group. The music had been turned down, and most of the partiers were passed out or had gone. A few still moved about, smoking and drinking.

On the large, marble porch, Aaron noticed Midnight Drifter's drummer, Bo, passed out on a large wicker chair.

Stopping at the bottom of the steps, Aaron knelt to the ground, trying to catch his breath. After a few seconds, he stood and stumbled to the van. Opening the back doors, he crawled in, then laid down and passed out; how much time passed after this he wasn't certain.

"Man, he must have drunk a keg. I've never seen Spyder this wiped out."

Aaron vaguely noticed Rick and Terry pulling him from the van and carrying him into his apartment. Once inside, they laid him on his bed. Barely aware of anything, he heard them talking.

"You think he'll be all right?" Rick asked.

"Sure, he just needs to sleep it off," Terry replied. Then, as Aaron drifted back into an unconscious state, the two left.

What seemed a long time later, Aaron woke enough to stand and make his way to the kitchen. He wasn't sure how long he had slept, but his mouth was dry. He held his head under the faucet and drank.

His vision was blurred, and he felt as if a truck had hit him. Stumbling to the small living room, he slumped down on the couch, facing the TV. He sat trying to catch his breath from the short walk.

As he stared at the TV, it began to light up. The picture was a fuzzy black-and-white. The familiar hissing sound accompanied the image of not being tuned into a station. As Aaron stared at the snowy image, his vision faded.

Seeming to slowly awaken, Aaron found himself sitting in front of a television, but he was in the recreation room of the second realm. He had not been here since his time in a coma.

Looking around, there was no one to be seen, but he could hear people outside. Struggling to stand, he walked over to the windows. Looking out, he saw many soldiers moving at double-time, as if in a hurry to reach a battle.

Turning around, Aaron found the captain standing in front of him. He tried to salute the officer, but his right arm came up painfully.

"Sir," he said as the captain returned the salute.

Looking over Aaron, the captain saw a battered warrior. Aaron's face had three large gashes that stretched from his forehead, across his nose and down the other side of his cheek. The wounds were open, though not bleeding.

Aaron's fatigues were tattered and ripped, indicating the fierce struggle he had faced. Along with many other cuts and injuries, his left arm appeared to be barely hanging on by a slim thread of skin.

"Are you all right, soldier?" the captain asked.

"Yes, sir, just a little winded," Aaron replied.

After saying this, his left arm fell completely off and landed on the floor with a thud.

Aaron glanced down at his arm, as did the captain. "Please, have a seat, soldier," the captain motioned to the chair in front of the television.

"What's going on out there, sir?" Aaron asked as he sat down.

The captain took a seat to the right of him, where he could see Aaron. "Your defeat of Locsheen has opened up an offensive opportunity. There are several fallen, along with lesser entities, that have trespassed into areas of the physical realm. They were emboldened by Locsheen's aggressive behavior.

"Now, with Locsheen's demise, we're successfully relocating these trespassers back into the second realm."

Aaron nodded wearily. Then he noticed several medics working on his wounds. They had seemingly appeared from nowhere.

"You should move to a place of rest. A place that you can recover." The captain paused, "When you feel better, you should work. Labor is good for the soul."

Aaron again nodded wearily. The captain smiled with compassion. Aaron's head bobbed from exhaustion as the medics dressed his wounds. Then one of the medics gave him a shot in what remained of his left arm. He became sleepy and faded back out.

Again, he wasn't sure how much time had passed by. He woke to someone knocking on the door of his small apartment. Looking up, he noticed the television was off.

The door opened, and Terry walked in. "Hey, Spyder. Where you been? Rick got worried. He asked me to stop by and see what's up on the way to the studio."

Terry sat down in a chair to the side of Aaron and looked him over.

"Dude, you look like hell! You been doing some of the hard stuff or what?"

Aaron stared with glazed eyes at Terry. "How long since the party?" he asked with a weak voice.

"Party? You mean Bitter Black's party?"

Aaron nodded.

"That was three days ago, man," Terry appeared puzzled. "You been out of it since the party?"

Aaron turned and stared at the television.

"Dude, you must have done some really heavy stuff." Terry then leaned back in the chair. He looked Aaron over again with an astonished expression. Then he seemed to think of something.

"Hey, did you hear about Lewis, the singer for Bitter Black?"

Aaron turned his head wearily and looked at Terry.

"No, I guess not if you've been out of it for the last three days." Terry then chuckled a little.

"Man, it's freaky as hell. His girlfriend found him on the floor of their room. She said the room looked like a train hit it. Anyway, she couldn't wake him up. Then the band came and finally got him awake. He was all wigged-out, like he wasn't sure who or where he was. The band just thought he had a bad trip or something.

"So, Lewis is acting all spazzed and shit. Then the next day, they go to the studio to rehearse. Lewis gets in front of the mic, and he starts singing like Mickey the doofus mouse!"

Terry laughed and leaning over, slapped Aaron on the leg.

"No, I'm serious dude. They said he sang like a chick from a cheer squad or something. The band was like, what the hell? And Lewis is acting like he's not even the same person.

"They tell him to stop acting like a dork, but he can't sing! So, the band gets all pissed off at him. Then yesterday, they go to Capstone's studio to lay down a track and guess what? Lewis still can't sing! He's seriously all washed up, and Capstone says to hell with the contract! It's crazy, man!

"So, now Bitter Black is all freaking out and shit, trying to find another singer. But Lewis is being a jerk about the whole thing and still trying to sing for them. Dude, it's all wacked out at Bitter Black's place."

Aaron gave a subtle nod. Silence held the room for a few seconds.

"I'm quitting Midnight Drifter, Terry," Aaron finally said with a flat voice.

The smile on Terry's face dropped off. "What? Man, that's a downer, Spyder. Why?"

"I'm tired," was all Aaron could say.

Terry studied Aaron for a minute. "Dude, you probably just need a break. You don't really want to quit, do you?"

"Yeah, I'm really quitting," Aaron replied.

Terry stood up. He scratched his head and seemed stressed. After looking around the living room, he appeared to think of something.

"Hey, let me fix you something to eat. You'll feel better. Besides, you got stuff at the studio. You can't just quit."

Aaron lowered his head and stared at the floor. "You can keep everything at the studio. I'll be leaving California right away."

Terry continued to examine Aaron. He winced a little, again seeming stressed. Then he went to the small kitchen. "I'll get you something to eat, Spyder. That'll help you feel better," he yelled out.

Then, glancing into the living room to be sure Aaron wasn't looking, he walked into Aaron's bedroom. Looking around, he found the battered notebook with Aaron's lyrics laying on the nightstand. Terry lifted his shirt and tucked the notebook in his pants, then pulled the shirt over it.

A few minutes later, Terry came from the kitchen with a bowl of cereal. He sat it on the end table beside Aaron. "Here you go, bro."

Terry moved to the side of Aaron but remained standing. "Man, I really hate to see you go, but if that's really what you want. You sure about your stuff at the studio?"

Aaron nodded wearily.

"Well, stop by before you leave, if you can. If not, I'll tell the guys. I'm sure they'll be bummed about it as well.

"I, uhm, well, I need to go, Spyder. Take care, all right?"

Aaron nodded again. Terry waved and then left.

The following morning, Aaron wearily climbed the steps of a bus and was soon headed back to Kansas.

CHAPTER THIRTEEN:

Affliction of Proximity

Aaron's parents were thrilled to have their son back home. Yet for several weeks, he stayed in his room, only coming out to eat or get cleaned up.

Eventually, Aaron did begin to walk around the expansive ranch. He would often sit and watch the sunrise or sunset.

After almost two months, he began working around the family land.

Three months after Aaron arrived home, his father drove a pickup out to a hayfield. He was shocked to find Aaron on a trailer, bucking large hay bales.

That evening, after supper, Jess walked out to the porch where his son sat. "I saw you working in the south hayfield today."

Aaron turned his attention to his father, who sat down in a chair beside him. A whippoorwill called out in the field. Aaron turned back to the horizon as the sun set and remained silent.

"Son, this is your ranch too. We have hired men to do the labor. You don't have to buck hay."

Aaron turned to his father. "Labor is good for the soul."

His dad nodded. "I'll not argue with that. But the Army doctors said you should take it easy on your back. You can drive the tractor or something. You don't have to do the heavy work."

Again, silence held the now-darkened porch. After a few seconds, Aaron spoke, "I need to work right now, Dad. I appreciate your concern, but I...," he paused, seeming to search for his words. Then he continued, "I just need to work. It's difficult for me to explain."

His dad nodded again.

"Is it a woman?" he asked.

Aaron turned and smiled a little. "It's... well, I'm just a little down in the spirit right now. I can't really explain it."

Though he still seemed puzzled by his son's behavior, Jess patted Aaron's leg and then went back inside.

As time went by, Aaron did, slowly, begin to move toward a supervisory position as opposed to the hard labor.

***

A little over a year after returning home, Aaron pulled up to where the ranch hands met in the morning. From there they would go out to the fields and mend fences or tend cattle.

As Aaron approached several men hanging around a pickup, he heard familiar music playing from the stereo inside. He moved closer to the pickup, stopped and listened with obvious interest.

The men turned around and waved at Aaron. Then the man who appeared to own the pickup, turned to Aaron, "Hey, boss! Betcha can't guess who this is."

Aaron listened for several more seconds. "That's Lowdown Showdown by Midnight Drifter."

The man and other ranch hands appeared both surprised and impressed. The man turned the stereo off and stepped out of the pickup, shutting the door behind him.

"How did you know that, boss?" the man asked.

"Oh, I heard it a year or so ago," Aaron replied, and then started toward a beat-up truck they used for going out to the fields.

The man expressed disbelief as he stepped up beside Aaron. "How did you do that? The record has only been out a few weeks."

Aaron opened the door on the old truck, and a squeaking sound came from the weathered vehicle. He sat his lunchbox in the front seat as the other ranch hands climbed in the back.

"Oh, well, maybe I was mistaken," Aaron replied.

The man stared at his boss in confusion but then scrambled to climb in the back as Aaron climbed in and started the old truck up.

***

Around two and a half years after Aaron had left Los Angeles, he and the ranch hands were returning from the fields. As the same old work truck pulled up to the men's vehicles, everyone noticed a large black limousine parked amongst the other pickups and cars. As the ranch hands spoke with excitement and pointed at the car, Aaron felt he knew who it was.

211

A few minutes later, he approached the luxury vehicle. The window rolled down, and Rengo smiled from inside. "Hello, Spyder. You have a few minutes to talk?"

Aaron smiled as well and got into the car.

"How have you been, Rengo?"

"I've been well, thank you. I hope you don't mind me visiting. I waited a long while before chancing a drive up here."

"No, I don't mind. I'm glad to see you."

Seeming to have prepared for the occasion, Rengo reached over and pulled a bottle of ginger ale from a small refrigerator beside him. He opened it and handed the drink to Aaron.

"After you left, I contacted several associates in Los Angeles. They eventually told me of the strange case concerning Bitter Black's lead singer. Seems they were on the verge of a large contract when the man completely lost his singing voice and stage presence."

Aaron downed a large drink of the soda. He nodded, "Yes, it was an odd thing."

Rengo smiled, "I can't imagine the struggle it must have been. I'm certain you did an invaluable service to mankind."

The two fell silent after Rengo said this. Then Aaron asked, "Sunny?"

Rengo readjusted himself and replied, "She has recently begun to date again."

"Good," Aaron said.

"And she has done remarkably well in the interior design business. My associate trained her for two years and then, with my indirect financial backing, helped her open her own business. She has turned that into a six-figure income for herself and has twenty-plus employees now."

Aaron smiled slightly, "Thank you. I appreciate you helping her."

"Well, actually it was not all my doing, and it is connected to the reason I'm here now."

Again, silence held the air for several long seconds. Then Rengo continued, "In a way, you played a large part in backing Sunny financially. It seems the singer of a band you may be familiar with, Midnight Drifter, began copyrighting the songs you wrote some years back. I didn't realize this until I heard one of their songs and recognized it as one you wrote.

"The singer copyrighted all of your songs over a two-year period. But he did so one at a time. When I copyrighted them, I simply put them in catalog form. It was a much easier and less expensive way to handle it.

"So, the singer for Midnight Drifter, as well as the band's record label, were quite surprised and shocked when I produced copyrights on the lyrics of virtually every song they've produced, making the singer's copyrights void and worthless. And they had already garnered two gold records by the time I realized they were using your songs."

Aaron took another drink of his soda but did smile a bit upon hearing this information. Rengo continued, "Perhaps needless to say, I was able to strike a very generous deal with the record company, and it was with this new stream of income that I financed Sunny's business."

Rengo then pulled a bank book from a pocket inside his suit. He handed it to Aaron.

"That's your share of the deal. As we agreed, fifty-fifty. Plus, future royalties will be deposited into that account until you make new arrangements."

Aaron sat his drink down and opened the bank book. His eyes widened as he scanned over the large figure.

"You're a wealthy man, Spyder."

Once again, only the subtle vibration of the limousine's engine filtered through the small interior.

"Thank you again," Aaron finally said.

"I still have your Plymouth, if you want it back."

"I'm afraid I sold the bike, dirt cheap. At the time I was in no condition to ride it back to Kansas."

"Oh, that's not a problem. I can buy another one should I want it."

Aaron nodded, "Well, thanks. I may come by your place and pick it up sometime."

"Yes, do come by, anytime."

Rengo paused as Aaron downed the last of his ginger ale. He then asked, "So, what are your plans now that you can do almost anything you wish?"

"I don't have any plans," Aaron replied meekly.

"You know, I thought that would be your answer. Though you may not have realized it, I did learn a few things from you. In fact, I very strongly felt I should do something for you."

As Rengo pulled open a pocket area on the side of his door, Aaron studied him curiously.

After retrieving a small binder, Rengo continued, "I know how you are about gifts. I... just felt I needed to get this one for you. Perhaps as a reward for a job well done. At any rate, I sensed I should get it for you."

Rengo handed the pocket binder to Aaron, who opened it and pulled several papers from it.

"What is it?" he asked, seeming baffled by the flyers and documents of various sizes and colors.

"It's an all-expenses-paid trip around Europe, in your name. I'm hoping you can pry yourself away from the cattle and hay long enough to redeem it."

This caused Aaron to chuckle, and his friend did as well.

Afterwards, Rengo stayed around the area for another week. He assisted Aaron in arranging his finances and prompted him to make several investments.

A month after Rengo's visit, Aaron found himself on a large ocean liner, cruising across the Atlantic. He leaned against the rail, the salty breeze caressed his hair and face as he admired the view.

He landed in Italy and spent several weeks visiting ancient Roman ruins and scenic countryside. Sitting at a table of a restaurant in the Italian alps, Aaron sipped his coffee and marveled at the snow-capped mountains.

Week after week, he moved around the ancient cities and historic sites of the European continent.

Several weeks later, Aaron sat in the British Museum of Art, London. He had been staring at a painting for half an hour. It was a painting by a renowned mystic artist, though few knew the artist to be a mystic.

Aaron had become lost in the marvelous work. He could clearly see the subtle spiritual aspects that most observers could not detect.

In almost silence, a shapely young woman moved beside the bench that Aaron sat on. She studied the painting for several minutes. The woman was around twenty-five years old. She had light brown hair that was cut in a fashionable bob.

She glanced over to Aaron, who had not moved the entire time. She then followed where his eyes were looking and again studied the painting, trying to detect what he was staring at.

For several more minutes, the young woman examined the painting. She turned and again studied Aaron to discover what had captured his attention so thoroughly.

Aaron was not aware of the young woman beside him. He was in a meditative state and didn't realize she was standing there and becoming rather captivated by his singular focus on this large painting.

For almost ten minutes, the young woman glanced back and forth to visualize what Aaron was seeing in the painting. She shifted her stance and even turned her head at various angles. She squinted her eyes more than once to gain insight.

Finally, unable to restrain herself, the young woman turned to Aaron and asked with a thick British accent, "What do you see?"

The question pulled Aaron from his trance-like state. He looked over to the young woman, who stood beside him with a puzzled expression.

He then said the first thing that came to his mind, "Something beautiful."

The woman expressed even more confusion, but then began to laugh. Aaron smiled and laughed a bit as well.

"That's either the most elaborate pick-up scheme I've ever been subjected to, or you're a rather interesting person. Which is it?"

With this question, the two began to talk. Soon the woman, whose name was Camilla, sat down beside Aaron.

After a lengthy discussion about renaissance artists, she invited him to have a cup of coffee with her. At the quaint corner coffeehouse, Aaron eventually asked Camilla out for dinner and she accepted.

As the two began to date, Aaron rented a small apartment and extended his stay in London.

Camilla had an accounting degree and worked for a prestigious firm in London. Aaron told her about his time in Vietnam and expressed his situation of receiving military disability. He also mentioned some investments but reserved his complete financial situation, and Camilla didn't press him to elaborate. She earned good wages and accepted that he was not in a situation to work at a regular job.

Soon, Aaron bought a bass guitar and began playing part-time at a recording studio. He earned a little money, but more importantly it gave him something to do.

Almost a year after they began to date, Aaron and Camilla were married. It was a small church ceremony with family and a few friends.

After the honeymoon, they began searching for a place to live. Though not passionate about "flat shopping," as Camilla called it, Aaron tried to seem enthused.

"Yes, it is nice. But I like the one we looked at Monday as well." The two walked around the apartment. Aaron nodded to Camilla and then scanned over a brochure with a headline reading, "St. James Apartments.",

"Yeah, it was all right, I guess." Aaron then examined the master bathroom again. This was their second look at these apartments.

"So, you really like this flat better?" Camilla asked.

"Well…" Aaron then expelled a long breath of air. "It is closer to your work. Plus, there's some nice shopping centers in this area, and, there's the park three blocks from here."

Camilla came over and took Aaron in her arms, "You know, I've heard it's useless to argue with a Yank."

The following week they began moving in.

***

A year later, Camilla gave birth to a baby girl. They named her Victoria, but Aaron was soon calling her Tori for short.

As the days passed by, Aaron's life began to revolve around his daughter. He seldom left her side and never left her in the care of anyone else. Camilla noticed the slightly domineering actions of her husband but generally dismissed them as attributable to Aaron being a new father.

Three years later, Aaron demanded their daughter's bed

remain close to he and Camilla's. He kept Tori within arm's reach almost twenty-four hours a day.

Though Camilla considered Aaron to be an overprotective father, she was unaware of what was occurring as her husband slept. While she lay beside Aaron, his dreams had slowly become invaded on a regular basis.

"You'll pay."

Aaron looked around to locate the source of the voice. He was in a dark place. He walked forward as a mist floated around him.

His left arm was missing; his face and body were riddled with scars from the battle with Locsheen.

"You'll pay for what you did."

Aaron sensed that he was dreaming, but it was not a physical dream. This was on the threshold of the spiritual realm. Somehow, he was being pulled to the borderline between the spiritual and physical realm.

Walking again, Aaron searched the mist apprehensively.

"You won't escape. I'll find you," the voice said again.

Then, Aaron spotted a brief glimpse of something. It had wings and looked like Locsheen.

As he moved through the mist, he suddenly heard his daughter call out, "Daddy!"

"Tori! Tori, where are you?" His pace quickened as he called out.

"Daddy!"

Then, he spotted Tori. He moved closer. Behind her, the frightening vision of Locsheen became clear. His eyes glowed red He held Tori and then laughed.

"TORI!" Aaron yelled out and sat up in bed.

Camilla sat up in shock. Aaron was sweating, his hand held out, as if reaching for something.

"What's going on?" Camilla asked.

Aaron moved over to Tori's bed. He picked her up and hugged her in his arms. She moaned and blinked her eyes sleepily, being half awake and half asleep.

"Are you all right?" Camilla asked.

"Yeah, I'm okay. I just… had a bad dream," he replied.

Later, he sat in the dark living room while Tori lay asleep in his arms.

As the weeks passed by, the nightmares grew in severity and frequency. Camilla increasingly became concerned.

"What's this?" She held a book up.

"It's a book," Aaron replied as he picked up Tori's empty cereal bowl.

"Demons and demonology? There's another in your office about vampires and werewolves. What are you getting into, Aaron?"

Taking the bowl over to the sink, he rinsed it out and sat it in the rack of the open dishwasher. Closing the door, he replied, "It's just some stuff I'm looking into. I was thinking of writing some stories." He then glanced back, as if to see her reaction.

Camilla still had a frightened expression. "I don't know what's going on with you these days. The nightmares are really becoming a problem, love. And reading this stuff won't help."

Pausing, she sat the book on an end table. Aaron walked over, picked Tori up and held her in his arms. Camilla continued, "I think you need some help. Can you look into some... doctors or therapists?"

Aaron remained silent as Camilla put her coat on, preparing to leave for work.

"You think I'm crazy?" he finally asked.

Picking up her purse, she expelled a long breath of air, then looked at him. "I'm… not sure what to think anymore."

Camilla then walked over and gave Tori a kiss.

"Bye, Mummy," she said.

"Bye, sweetie."

Camilla then left for work.

"Is Mummy mad at you, Daddy?"

Sitting her down on the large rug in the living room, Aaron turned the television on.

"She may be a little upset, but it's all right, sweetheart."

After tuning in a children's show, Aaron retrieved the book from the end table and began reading, as his daughter watched TV.

The following day, he took Tori to the park, as he did several times a week. As he was sitting her in the swing, she asked, "Do you know Mr. Black Jacket, Daddy?"

Aaron studied her for a few seconds. "What are you talking about?"

"The man that comes to the park when we do. I call him Mr. Black Jacket. Do you know him?"

Aaron turned and looked over the park. There was no man wearing a black jacket around.

"What man are you talking about?"

"He's not here now, Daddy."

Aaron stood and looked all around the park again. He then took Tori from the swing, and they walked home.

As they entered the lobby of their apartment building, they met Mrs. Humphrey, who lived on the first floor.

"Hello, Mr. Prescott. And hello, Victoria. Would you two like some tea and cookies?"

"Hello, Mrs. Humphrey. I'm sorry but not this morning." He then led Tori to the elevator.

That afternoon, Camilla walked into the house to find Aaron watching out the window.

As the days went by, Aaron would watch out the window more and more. When they went somewhere, he would hold onto Tori and almost refuse to let her go until they were back in their apartment.

On one occasion, he was shopping for groceries. As he pushed Tori around the store in the cart, he noticed her lean over and wave to someone.

Looking back, Aaron saw no one. "Who did you wave to?"

"Mr. Black Jacket. Sometimes he's at the store when we go shopping. He waves at me."

Aaron pushed the cart around the store several times in search of the man. When he couldn't find the mysterious Mr. Black Jacket, he abandoned the cart of groceries, and taking Tori in his arms, he left.

"What about our groceries, Daddy?"

Glancing behind him, Aaron replied, "We'll come back later."

When they were back home, Aaron sat Tori down on the couch.

"Sweetie, this Mr. Black Jacket, is he real?"

Tori's head twisted a bit as she thought of her father's question. "I think he's real, Daddy. How do I know if he's not real?"

Aaron smiled and caressed his daughter's cheek. "Well, it's just that sometimes children have imaginary friends."

"Is Mr. Black Jacket a... magenary friend, Daddy?"

Aaron smiled again and stood up. "It's nothing to worry about, sweetie. I'll get some cartoons on for you."

Once again, when Camilla came home from work, she found Aaron watching out the window.

It came to a head one night as they slept. Again, Aaron found himself on the border of the physical and spiritual realm. Moving through a mist-filled jungle, he followed the cries of Tori. Sweat trickled down the side of his head. He was in his pajamas. He pushed a leafy bush. The dream was so real that Aaron sat up in bed while still asleep, climbed out and began walking toward the living room.

"Are you all right?" Camilla asked sleepily as he moved in a mechanical manner toward the door. Sensing something was not right, Camilla climbed out of bed and followed her husband. In the middle of the living room, she found Aaron standing in the dark, staring blankly at the windows. Camilla stood in front of her husband and waved her hand in front of his face.

Aaron didn't see his wife. In his dream, he had walked to an open area. There he found the fallen angel, Locsheen, who stood holding a crying Tori in front of him. His deadly claws were extended, as if ready to slice the girl apart.

"Let her go," Aaron said.

Camilla stepped back when Aaron said this. "Let who go?" she asked.

Again, Aaron heard nothing his wife said.

Locsheen let out a hollow laugh. "You'll pay, Spyder. You'll pay for what you did."

Aaron glanced down at Tori, then back to Locsheen. "You're dead," he said.

"Who's dead?" Camilla asked, eyes widening.

"You're dead. I destroyed you," Aaron said, still staring blankly at the window.

Camilla stepped back again. She stared with fear at her husband.

"Who's dead? Who did you destroy?" she almost shouted.

Locsheen again laughed in a low and aggressive tone. Then he became as mist. Aaron now heard Camilla and, upon waking, almost fell to the ground.

Staggering to remain on his feet and understand where he was, he heard Camilla almost shout again, "Who did you destroy? What are you talking about, Aaron? What's going on?"

"What do you mean? I... I must have been dreaming."

Camilla began to cry. She shook her head and put her hand to her mouth. "I don't know what's going on with you. I can't take this anymore. I can't stay here and allow our daughter to be around this."

"Camilla, listen!"

She walked into the bedroom and began to get dressed.

"Camilla, please listen, it's just… stuff, from battles… from way back. It's just dreams."

Though he continued to beg, his pleas went unheeded as she threw some clothes in a bag and, taking Tori from her bed, moved quickly out the door, almost slamming it in Aaron's face.

As the sun rose and broke in through the windows, Aaron sat in the living room, staring blankly into space.

For three days, he barely ate or drank. Whiskers took over his face as he mulled about the apartment in a daze.

Five days after Camilla left with Tori, Aaron sat in front of the television. It had been playing all day, though he was barely aware of it. It was almost 1:00 in the morning.

The station announced the day's programming had come to an end. There was a test screen for several seconds, and the station went completely off the air. A snowy haze took over the TV, and a fuzzy sound streamed from the large console television.

As Aaron stared at the screen, he drifted into a meditative state. Moments later, he found himself in the spiritual realm. He sat in the recreation room staring at the television.

Glancing down at himself, he found that his left arm was again missing, the sleeve of his uniform pinned up, indicating the condition of his spiritual self. He now wore a crisp dress uniform as opposed to the battle fatigues he had worn before.

Standing up, he felt a warm breeze blow through the open windows. Looking toward them, he saw that the curtains were tattered and torn, as if weathered by years of exposure in the wind.

As he walked around the recreation room, he noticed that everything appeared neglected and unused. The pool table had a layer of dust on it. He picked up a pool cue and the outline of the stick remained distinctive.

Moving through the barracks hallway, he glanced into an open door. It had once housed a mystic warrior that he was quite fond of and had spent many hours studying with. Now the soldier's room was empty and had obviously been so for a long time.

There seemed to be no one anywhere. Aaron moved on.

At the entrance, a small desk sat unattended. Where a lower-ranking soldier normally recorded activities, only a parched and weathered notebook lay unattended.

Turning into a doorway, Aaron jogged up two flights of stairs to his room. The door to his quarters was open, as it was on many other rooms of the vacant building.

Another breeze flowed past him as he crept inside. Moving over to the open windows, he looked out. The barracks next door also stood silent and lifeless. Below, the sidewalk held none of the busy soldiers it had before.

Turning, Aaron examined his bunk. Moving over to it, he patted it lightly and dust floated up into the air.

Noticing the doors were cracked open on his locker, he stepped over to it. Opening the two doors wide, he saw that his battle fatigues and various clothes were barely hanging by threads to the rusty coat hangers.

He reached in and pulled a set of battle fatigues out, and the cloth almost disintegrated. The fatigues fell from the hanger and to the bottom of the locker.

As he closed one of the locker doors, he found himself face to face with the captain. Though shocked, he wasn't frightened. The captain smiled slightly. Aaron came to attention and saluted his leader.

After a casual return salute, the captain said, "Let's walk."

Aaron followed him down the stairs and outside. At the end of the barracks, there was a bench. The captain motioned for Aaron to sit and he did. After sitting beside Aaron, the captain turned to him.

"Where is everyone?" Aaron asked.

The captain took in a deep breath. He exhaled and replied, "Most from your group are no longer in this fight. The war is the same, but the battles have changed, as battles always do. The enemy has once again altered its tactics."

Aaron looked down at the ground. The captain continued, "Life in the physical realm is fleeting. They served a higher purpose. They continue in the spiritual realm. The ones that throw away their opportunity to grow spiritually and live on are the ones we mourn. Not the brave spirit warriors that sacrifice so others may have a chance."

Aaron nodded and gazed out at the vacant buildings. A small tumbleweed rolled by. The captain then asked, "But you're not here looking for your comrades, are you?"

Aaron slowly shook his head.

"The shadow of The Defiler has fallen on me. I wasn't prepared for it. The nature of his shadow is more frightening than anything I've faced. My dreams are haunted by the safety of my daughter."

Silence held the air for several long seconds. Aaron looked at the captain. He expressed compassion.

"Sometimes, the last miles are the most difficult to travel," the captain said.

After some thought and a deep breath, Aaron replied, "My wife doesn't understand what's happening. She's taken our daughter. I don't know where they are, and I don't know what I'd tell her if I did know where they were."

The captain nodded in understanding.

"You've been faithful in a most difficult task. Those in the physical realm don't see or understand the wounds and scars received in spiritual battles."

Aaron nodded again. He took in another deep breath, "I can't lose them. I don't believe I could go on without them."

A breeze moved through as Aaron looked out, seeming to contemplate being without Tori and Camilla.

After a few seconds of thought, his leader said, "Mark my words, you'll not be alone at the end." The captain patted Aaron's shoulder, then stood up and walked away.

Aaron sat for a while. He then went back to the recreation room. After staring at the snowy screen of the television, he faded out.

Aaron wasn't sure how long he slept, but when he woke, morning sunshine crept into the apartment. He could hear the lock on the door clicking behind him.

Standing up and turning toward the doorway, he saw it

open, then Tori quickly walked in. Spotting her father, she shouted for joy and ran to him, "Daddy!!"

Aaron knelt to catch her in his arms. Tears immediately welled up in his eyes and began to stream down his cheeks as he held Tori.

Camilla walked in and looking down at the two, smiled in an apprehensive way.

"She was driving me completely mad," his wife said.

Turning to Tori, Aaron said, "Good job!"

CHAPTER FOURTEEN:

Verdict

Afterwards, Aaron and Camilla spoke. She said that she understood Aaron had been in the war and must have done stuff he didn't want to talk about. But he had to promise her, if the nightmares grew worse, he would seek help.

Aaron agreed.

The dreams did continue, but Aaron managed to control himself and hide the severity of them from Camilla.

He continued to guard Tori and rarely allowed her to be very far from him. He also seldom wanted to go far from their apartment and, to Camilla's frustration, was always in a hurry to get back home when they did go somewhere.

Three months after Camilla and Tori returned, Aaron and his daughter were walking home from the park.

As they approached their apartment building, Tori suddenly stopped and said, "Daddy, my shoe has come unlaced."

Aaron glanced down. "Oh, well, let's go inside, and I'll tie it back."

He picked Tori up and carried her past the sign and into the building.

Rather than going to the elevator, he turned right and sat Tori on a bench in the hall. As he kneeled to tie her shoe, five men walked into the apartment entrance and moved toward the elevator. They were dressed in dark suits, and the one in the middle wore dark glasses and a long black coat.

As the men moved past the hall where Aaron was tying Tori's shoe, the crucifix necklace Rengo had given Aaron years before popped out from his shirt.

Tori giggled, "Daddy, your necklace just jumped out!"

Aaron glanced down at the crucifix necklace that had once belonged to another Tori.

"You mean, it fell from my shirt?"

"No, Daddy, it jumped out! Isn't that queer?"

Aaron's face hardened a bit as he considered his daughter's comment. He finished tying the shoe and then put the necklace back into his shirt. They then stood and went to the elevator.

After moving up to the fifth floor, the doors opened and, the two stepped out. Then Aaron froze in place.

In the hallway, standing in front of his apartment door was August Rollins and four men.

The elevator doors closed behind Aaron. He stepped back, pulling Tori to the now closed elevator doors. August turned to Aaron.

"That's him," he said and immediately the four men reached into their coats and pulled pistols, with silencers attached.

Aaron moved Tori behind him. She began to cry from the sight of men pulling out guns.

"Essene! What a surprise... for you!"

August took several steps toward Aaron. The four men followed on both sides of him, holding their pistols pointed at Aaron.

"You're a hard man to find, Essene. It's taken me years to track you down. Fortunately for me, I have a connection with your travel agency in New Orleans. You really should have ordered your 'European escape' from a different resource, Mr. Prescott."

"What do you want?" Aaron asked.

"What do I want?" the vampire laughed.

"Do you see this?" August pulled his darkened glasses down and pointed to his forehead. Though it would be unseen by others, Aaron could clearly see a large and unsightly scar from the drop of whiskey he had poured on August years ago.

"YOU SEE IT?" August shouted.

"You do see it, don't you? I see it everyday. I've looked at it for years. And I've been forced to look at it through glasses. My eyes have never completely recovered. These scars have brought my blood to a boil time and time again. They've brought me here to settle a score. Just as I swore to you, I would do."

August put his glasses back on and then glanced down to Tori as she peeked around her father's leg.

"But you. You're inept and frail now, Essene. I've heard how you've become naive and reckless. Did you really think I would just forget about what you did to me? You must have thought I would have forgiven you by now. That's why you

232

thought it would be safe to take a wife. And look there, such a healthy young offspring too."

Aaron stepped closer to the elevator, moving Tori with him.

"YOU LEAVE HER ALONE! You better not lay a finger on her, August. I swear, I'll…"

"You'll what, Essene? What will you do? You've become impotent and pathetic. I was told about your playtime in the park… your, hours spent in the library and grocery shopping. At first, I didn't believe it. The once formidable Spyder Bones playing in the park with his cute little child.

"Well, now it's all over for you, Essene. And when I'm through with you, I'll take your daughter and slowly suck the life out of her over a period of ten or fifteen years."

After August said this, the doors on the elevator opened. Aaron moved Tori inside and hitting the button said, "Go to Mrs. Humphrey's room, quickly!"

As the doors closed, Aaron stepped away from the elevator, holding his arms up to shield any possible shots from August's men. The vampire's face twisted with anger. But he quickly recovered.

"It doesn't matter. I'll stop and pick her up on the way out. I may even have your wife brought to me. She appears to be bubbling over with the sweet essence of life. I'll feed on her and your daughter both, while you rot in the ground."

Aaron lowered his arms as the elevator chimed out that it had landed on the first floor.

"I've waited a long time to watch you die, Essene. And I assure you, it will be painful. My men will start with your legs and slowly work their way up. But you may plead for mercy now. I will listen. Do you wish to ask for my mercy? Perhaps I'll spare you some pain."

"No," Aaron replied.

"Very well, Essene, good-bye." As August said this, the four men cocked their pistols.

"Good-bye, August. I'm relieved it's finally over."

The vampire chuckled, "You're relieved that your life is over?"

"I'm relieved my task is over, and I'll finally be able to rest."

August appeared puzzled. "Your task?"

"You, August. You're my task. There are consequences for exceeding the boundary's set forth by the creator."

When Aaron said this, August's face became pale, as if recalling a long-lost memory. He then appeared to be retracing the events that led him to where he was. He suddenly recalled the apartments were named "St. James Apartments." His face expressed a sudden panic.

"You know the rules, don't you? Perhaps it's been a century or two since you heard them, but you know the rules." Aaron then spoke in Greek, "Συνέπειες της υπέρβασης του τερματικού σταθμού."

A breeze flowed through the hall. The light above the elevator door went out. August grimaced, as if in pain. Panic continued to stretch over his face.

"SHOOT HIM! SHOOT HIM NOW!!"

The men pulled the triggers on their pistols; only a clicking sound was heard.

234

The locks on the apartment doors began clicking from Aaron all the way down the hall and past August.

The vampire looked around, seeming very frightened as each door lock clicked one by one.

Aaron closed his eyes and lowered his head. He began to speak in Aramaic.

"KILL HIM! KILL HIM NOW!" August shouted.

The four men started toward Aaron. He raised his head and opened his eyes; a bright light shone from them. August let out a yell of pain and raised his arms to deflect the light. The four men fell on the floor unconscious.

A voice erupted from Aaron's mouth. It was the distinct and authoritative voice of the captain.

"August Rollins, The Defiler. You have breached the boundary of laws set forth by our creator. By the authority allowed me from the divine, I pass long overdue judgment upon your soul."

August began to plead, "Michael! Michael, please have mercy, please... Michael!"

Aaron's arms began to raise by his side, as if summoning a great power. He began to radiate light from head to toe.

August cowered in the illumination. He writhed in pain.

"The time of mercy has long past, Defiler. Your judgment is death."

A brilliant light burst from Aaron. It swept through the entire hall, and as August screamed and held his hands up, the light slowly disintegrated his entire being.

The light then dissipated. Aaron leaned forward, seeming to deflate, and then dropped to his knees.

As he slumped over facing the floor, the locks began to click open. The light over the elevator came back on, and several people stepped out of their rooms, only to find four men unconscious on the floor and Aaron, appearing exhausted.

He staggered to his feet and pushed the button on the elevator. As the doors opened, he stumbled in and pushed the button for the first floor.

When the doors opened on the ground floor, Aaron practically fell out. As he stepped around the corner toward Mrs. Humphrey's, sirens of police cars could be heard screaming up to the hotel.

Knocking on the door, he said, "Mrs. Humphrey, it's me, Mr. Prescott."

The lock unlatched, and the door opened. Tori immediately ran into her father's arms. "DADDY, I was so scared for you, Daddy!"

Aaron kissed her head as a few tears rolled down his cheeks.

Tori pulled back and looked at her father. "Is the bad man gone, Daddy?"

Aaron smiled. "Yes, sweetheart, the bad man is finally gone. He'll never bother us again."

The End

We hope you enjoyed Spyder Bones by Oliver Phipps. For your convenience we've listed some additional Oliver Phipps books below, which you may also enjoy. For a complete list of Oliver's works, please check online or visit www.oliverphipps.com.

The House on Cooper Lane: Based on a True Story

It's 1984 and all Bud Fisher wants to do is find a place to live in Madison, Louisiana. With his dog, Badger, they come across a beautiful old mansion that was converted into apartments.

Something should have felt odd when he found out nobody lived in any of the apartments. To make matters worse, the owner is reluctant to let him rent one. Eventually he negotiates an apartment in the historic old house, but soon finds out that he's not quite as alone as he thought. What ghostly secret has the owner failed to share?

It's up to Bud to unravel the mysteries of the upstairs apartments, but is he really ready to find out the truth?

A Tempest Soul

Seventeen-year-old Gina Falcone has been alone for much of her life. Her father passed away while she was young. Her unaffectionate mother eventually leaves her to care for herself when she is only thirteen.

Though her epic journey begins by an almost deadly mistake, Gina will find many of her heart's desires in the most unlikely of places. The loss of everything is the catalyst that brings her to an unimagined level of accomplishment in her life.

Yet Gina soon realizes the same events that brought her success may also bring everything crashing down around her. The new life she has built soon beckons for something she left behind. Now, the new woman must find a way to dance through a life she could have never dreamed of.

Where the Strangers Live

When a passenger plane disappears over the Indian Ocean in autumn 2013, a massive search gets underway.

A deep trolling, unmanned pod picks up faint readings, and soon the deep-sea submersible Oceana and her three crew members are four miles below the ocean surface in search of the black box from flight N340.

Nothing could have prepared the submersible crew for what they discover and what happens afterward. Ancient evils and otherworldly creatures challenge the survival of the Oceana's crew. Mysteries of the past are revealed, but death hangs in the balance for Sophie, Troy and Eliot in this deep-sea science fiction thriller.

Twelve Minutes till Midnight

A man catches a ride on a dusty Louisiana road only to find out he's traveling with notorious outlaws Bonnie and Clyde.

The suspense is nonstop as confrontation settles in between a man determined to stand on truth and an outlaw determined to dislocate him from it.

"Twelve Minutes till Midnight will take you on an unforgettable ride."

Diver Creed Station

Wars, disease and a massive collapse of civilization have ravaged the human race a hundred years in the future. Finally, in the late twenty-second century, mankind slowly begins to struggle back from the edge of extinction.

When a huge 'virtual life' facility is restored from a hibernation type of storage and slowly brought back online, a new hope materializes.

Fragments of humanity begin to move into the remnants of Denver and the Virtua-Gauge facilities, which offer seven days of virtual leisure for seven days work in this new and growing social structure.

Most inhabitants of this new lifestyle begin to hate the real world and work for the seven-day period inside the virtual pods. It's the variety of luxury roleplay inside the virtual zone that supply's the incentive needed to work hard for seven days in the real world.

In this new social structure, a man can work for seven days in a food dispersal unit and earn seven days as a twenty-first century software billionaire in the virtual zone. As time goes by and more of the virtual pods are brought back online, life appears to be getting better.

Rizette and her husband Oray are young technicians that settle into their still new marriage as the virtual facilities expand and thrive.

Oray has recently attained the level of a Class A Diver and enjoys his job. The Divers are skilled technicians that perform critical repairs to the complex system from inside the virtual zone.

His title of Diver originates from often working in the secure "lower levels" of the system. These lower-level areas are the dividing space between the real world and the world of the virtual zone. When the facility was built, the original designers intentionally placed this buffer zone in the programming to avoid threats from non-living virtual personnel.

As Oray becomes more experienced in his elite technical position as a Diver, he is approached by his virtual assistant and forced to make a difficult decision. Oray's decision triggers events that soon pull him and his wife, Rizette, into a deadly quest for survival.

The stage becomes a massive and complex maze of virtual

world sequences, as escape or entrapment hang on precious threads of information.

System ghosts from the distant past intermingle with mysterious factions that have thrown Oray and Rizette into a cyberspace trap with little hope for survival.

Ghosts of Company K: Based on a True Story

Tag along with young Bud Fisher during his daily adventures in this ghostly tale based on actual events. It's 1971 and Bud and his family move into an old house in northern Arkansas. Bud soon discovers they live not far from a very interesting cave as well as a historic Civil War battle site. As odd things start to happen, Bud tries to solve the mysteries. But soon the entire family experiences a haunting situation.

If you enjoy ghost tales based on true events, then you'll enjoy Ghosts of Company K. This heartwarming story brings the reader into the life and experiences of a young boy growing up in the early 1970s. Seen through innocent and unsuspecting eyes, Ghosts of Company K reveals a haunting tale from the often-unseen perspective of a young boy.

Bane of the Innocent

"There's no reason for them to shoot us; we ain't anyone." - Sammy, Bane of the Innocent.

Two young boys become unlikely companions during the fall of Atlanta. Sammy and Ben somehow find themselves, and each other, in the rapidly changing and chaotic environment of the war-torn Georgia city.

As the siege ends and the fall begins in late August and early September of 1864, the Confederate troops begin to move out, and Union forces cautiously move into the city. Ben and Sammy simply struggle to survive, but in the process, they develop a friendship that will prove more important than either one could imagine.

A Life Naive

Life for twenty-seven-year-old Hershel Lawson has been relatively uneventful and that's the way he likes it. When his grandmother passes away, leaving him her car and a last wish of him taking her ashes to L.A., his life takes a turn, and it will never be the same again.

With his new task and his grandmother's ashes, Hershel sets out from St. Louis, Missouri, in the spring of 1962. He travels unimpeded along scenic Route 66 for two days but is suddenly and unexpectedly relieved of two important things, his car and his wallet.

Sally is a sassy and street-smart young woman on her way to Hollywood. She's determined to prove everyone wrong in the one-horse town she left and make it as an actress in California. Through mishaps of her own, Sally comes across Hershel.

Though neither one realizes it, the real journey is about to begin.

Take a seat and journey with Hershel and Sally along historic Route 66 during its heyday. Laugh and maybe shed a tear or two as they struggle against the odds, and often each other, to make it a few more miles down the highway.

The Bitter Harvest

The year is 1825, and a small Native American village has lost many of its people and bravest warriors to a pack of Lofa; huge beasts humanoid in shape but covered with coarse hair. The creatures are taller than any normal man and fiercer than even the wildest animal.

Rather than leave the land of their ancestors, the tribe chooses to stay and fight the beasts. But they're losing the war, and perhaps more critically, they're almost without hope.

The small community grasps for anything to help them survive. There is a warrior on the frontier known as Orenda. He's already legendary across the west for his bravery and honor.

Onsi, a young villager, sets out on a journey to find the warrior.

Orenda will be forced to choose between almost certain death, not just for himself, but also his warrior wife, Nazshoni, and her brother, Kanuna, or a dishonorable refusal that would mean annihilation for the entire village.

The crucial decision is only the beginning, and Orenda will soon face the greatest test of his life; the challenge that could turn out to be too much even for a warrior of legend.

*

www.ingramcontent.com/pod-product-compliance
Lightning Source LLC
Chambersburg PA
CBHW070917180626
46817CB00003B/1100